Linnette, The Lioness

The Real Duchesses of London

LINNETTE, THE LIONESS

LAVINIA KENT

AVONIMPULSE

This book is a work of fiction. The characters, incidents, and dialogue are drawn from the author's imagination and are not to be construed as real. Any resemblance to actual events or persons, living or dead, is entirely coincidental.

EPub Edition July 2011 ISBN: 9780062107930

Print Edition ISBN: 9780062115706

10 9 8 7 6 5 4 3 2 1

Kathryn, The Duchess of Harrington

"I am the perfect duchess. I am beautiful, rich, well read, well spoken, and have a civilized relationship with the duke. What more could a woman want?"

Elizabeth, The Countess of Westhampton

"I may not be a duchess, but I am more of a lady than any of them. You'll never see me in the scandal sheets. Mind you, I am not saying I haven't ever been scandalous—just that you'll never know."

Georgianna, Lady Richard Tennant

"My son will be a duke. It doesn't matter if I get to be a duchess as long as I know my son will inherit from his uncle, will hold the title. My husband may have broken many of his promises to me, but that one is absolute."

Linnette, The Dowager Duchess of Doveshire

"I have no intention of giving up what is mine. I've run the house and the estates for years. Why would I ever give them up now? I don't care who the new duke is."

Annabelle, The Marchioness of Tattingstong

*"They say that, because I am American, I have no taste,
no grace, no style, no refinement. I have every intention
of showing them just how wrong they are—and when
the time comes I will be the perfect duchess."*

*All quotes as relayed to Miss Jane White, more or perhaps less
accurately, by Miss Mary White, lady's maid for the Duchess of
Harrington

THE MAIDS

Jane White, newly hired upstairs maid in the house of Lady Smythe-Burke, resisted the urge to twirl as she strolled down the street. It was her first half-day in the week she'd been at her new employment. Normally a maid had to wait a full fortnight to be given a half-day, but her employer apparently had some modern ideas and Jane certainly wasn't going to complain.

She'd arranged to take the same half-day as her friend Abby Dobbs and the two women were going to walk through the park and enjoy the early summer air. Jane had even grabbed some bread crusts from the kitchen in anticipation of their treat. There was nothing like feeding the ducks to complete an afternoon of laughter and frivolity—maybe they'd even see that footman she'd had her eye on.

Jane paused for a moment at the apothecary just down the street from her former employer. There were a couple of new cartoons and prints in the window. She hurried up to the glass eagerly.

"Ooh, is that another one in the window?" Abby's voice called to Jane from behind, causing Jane to step away from the shop's large window.

"Do you mean the one of the Dowager Duchess of Doveshire? I am surprised you haven't seen it before. This one is mean—just like the last couple. And not nearly as well drawn—not like that first one with all the duchesses. Do you really think the dowager duchess could have one in the oven? And to say that the father is a married man! My sister, Mary, saw her last week at Harrington House and didn't say anything about her belly. She is young enough, but I've never heard that she wants to marry again," Jane responded, her thoughts returning to the pleasure of the day to come. She wondered if she had enough pocket change for some fresh chestnuts. They were more fun in the winter but she had a hankering.

"But who's the gentleman? Do you think his shoulders are really that wide?"

"He's the Duke of Harrington. That's what makes this one so awful. I believe he loves his duchess—I think I even saw a different print of him making lovey eyes at her. I'd tell you some of the things my sister has whispered to me but they are too shocking. I can't believe that he'd have a child with another woman. If he is the father, I think that's just horrible."

"No," Abby said. "I saw that one days ago. Look more closely. The cartoon is almost the same, but this time it's a different man. The pose is the same, and it looks like he's wearing a ducal cornet, but it's not Harrington. This one looks like a man who's worked hard in his life."

Jane peered more closely, thoughts of chestnuts forgotten. "Oh my, I see what you mean. No, I don't know who he is. Maybe Mary will know."

"Why would they show the dowager duchess with two different men? Do you think she's been sleeping with both?"

"I told you I don't believe she was sleeping with Harrington—although it would be a good bit of gossip if she was. Can you imagine two men?"

"I have trouble when I even think about one. Cook always says that's what men are—trouble."

Jane thought about her handsome footman. Lady Smythe-Burke did like a footman with a well-shaped leg. "You may be right about that. And," she turned to look more closely at the print, "I would like to know who he is. You are right about the coronet—hmm, what duke aren't we thinking of? I thought I'd learned them all by sight—at least the way they look in cartoons."

Abby suddenly grew very still. She turned to Jane with wide eyes. "You don't suppose he could be . . ."

CHAPTER ONE

"I am not with child."

The words struck James before he'd even walked across the entrance hall of the house. The door to the south parlor swung open and Linnette, the Dowager Duchess of Doveshire—and his secret lover—stood and stared at him. She must have seen him arrive.

As always, his breath caught when he saw her. Even now, shimmering with rage, she was the most incredible thing he'd ever seen. Her coppery hair glinted in the morning light and her face was flushed. Her dark emerald eyes shone with more life than anyone he'd ever known. Her tightly pursed lips drew even tighter as she stared at him. She took another step forward, her grace almost feline, but not some tame house cat. No, Linnette moved like a lioness, strong, powerful, and sure—and very angry.

Despite her anger, his body, as always, responded to her very presence. The desire grew to sweep her into his arms to kiss all her troubles away.

"I repeat, I am not with child," she said again, waiting for his response.

"I don't believe I ever said you were," he answered with considered calm.

She glared a second longer, then with her skirts flapping like a sail in the wind, she turned and stormed back into the parlor.

What now? This was certainly not what he had hoped and expected when he had received Linnette's note that morning. The note, summoning him far before normal visiting hours, had given him very definite hopes—hopes that seemed doomed to disappointment. Eight years ago, before he'd left, he'd known her every nuance: now he felt lost in a strange land. He might know her body, but her mind remained a mystery.

He paused one more second, drew a deep breath, and walked into the parlor.

He stepped slightly aside as he entered. Linnette had a temper to match her hair and he'd learned to be careful of it almost two decades ago. She'd had a propensity to throw things as a girl, and had always had the most wicked aim.

"I am not with child." Linnette repeated the words with even more vigor. She stormed back and forth across the room, hands on hips. She was fully dressed in a morning gown of flowered yellow muslin, but her glowing hair was still unbound, loose about her shoulders. Clearly, she was not quite herself at the moment, but then she hadn't been herself since—

Damnation, he knew what this was about—and it wasn't about anything he would wish to discuss. And why had she summoned him about it?

"This is because of that cartoon again, isn't it?" he asked, his voice as soothing as he could manage. He knew how deeply hurt she'd been by the cartoon that shown her heavily pregnant. She'd never been a woman to court scandal—even with him. "The one of you and the Duke of Harrington that appeared a week ago. I know you must find it distressing, but I believed what you said about all your interviews involving the building of railroads and canals and have never even considered that you might be bearing his child." He stepped forward, reaching out a hand to catch her arm, to hold her still—it was difficult to talk to a woman who seemed determined to cross the room a hundred times in less than a minute. She did not throw off his hand, stepping nearer to him if anything. His fingers warmed against her soft flesh and he fought the urge to pull her closer. She smelled of musk this morning, something womanly and mysterious. He wished he could pull her yet nearer, distract her from her displeasure. He gave a gentle tug.

She did not move. "No. Its not about that one—and you are right I am certainly not bearing Harrington's child." She held still beneath his touch, but he could feel the anxiety and anger that coursed through her. She turned her face up to his, her skin bare of powder, her light freckles showing. Her jade eyes shone with even more emotion than usual, her lips pale, their centers reddened as if she'd been biting them all morning.

"Then what is this about? Are you finally ready to talk about what—No, I see from your look that you are not. Why don't you sit and tell me why you have summoned me?" He gestured to the dainty chaise under one of the high, heavily draped windows. The faster he got her calmed, the sooner—his gaze slid toward the hallway, his thoughts traveling up the stairs. It was an unlikely occurrence, but his body definitely approved of the idea. "It must be something quite important for you to summon me at such an early hour."

"This is important—and it is about us. I cannot believe you do not already know. I was sure everyone would know by now. My maid told me with my breakfast—not that I could eat after—." She pulled from his grasp and began to pace again. "I cannot believe this. After everything that has happened—now this."

What on earth was she talking about? A sudden thought took him. "Did you miss your courses? Is that why you are talking about being with child? Is that why you are acting this way?" He dodged as she turned and swung at him. She was slight compared to himself, but even as a ten-year-old she'd packed a good punch.

"You are such a man. Every time I am emotional it must have something to do with my being a woman. And if I'd missed my courses I wouldn't be saying I was not with child. Do you really think that I'd believe everybody knew about my courses?"

That required fast thought. He wished he knew how to help her. Although he was the last person she seemed to want help from. "I imagine your maid does—didn't you mention your maid?"

Linnette stormed to the window and stared down at the street. He could see her magnificent chest rise as she pulled in a deep breath, her breasts straining against the fine muslin.

"I am sorry," he said. "I would confess I had other thoughts on my mind when I arrived. I am quite baffled by why you would have summoned me at this hour. I should have taken the time to listen." The sentiment was heartfelt, but he also knew that an apology was the fastest way to calm her and to find out what had happened.

She turned back to him, her eyes steady, considering his words. Her lips were still quivering with emotion and he found his eyes drawn to them. They were so full, so lush, so inviting, so—damn, Linnette was right—he was such a man, and as a man he could not help his thoughts straying out the door and up the stairs. Linnette with her fury spinning about her was more arousing than anything he'd encountered since—since longer than he could remember. He longed for the chance to give her another way to expend all that energy. He shifted, easing his trousers, as he forced his eyes back up to her eyes. It wouldn't do to be caught staring at her mouth, his thoughts plain on his face.

"I am sorry also," she said after a moment. "I am upset and I should have explained why before reacting in such a fashion. I should not take out my anger upon you." She walked to the small table that stood under the window. Picking up a single sheet of cheap paper she turned toward him. "My maid brought it to me this morning. I wish I did not need to show it to you. I wish it did not exist at all. Things are already complicated enough between us."

He reached out to take the paper. "Is it more foolishness about you and Harrington? Nobody would be fool enough to believe it. Have you seen the way he's been looking at his duchess these last days? I think there's even a print of the two of them looking like lovebirds. A man with that look on his face is not involved with another woman—not even one as ravishing as you."

"Oh, stop flattering me and look at the damned thing."

Letting his eyes drop to the paper, he froze. Bloody hell. No wonder Linnette was so upset.

He walked over to the window so that the sun was full on the paper and stared down at the cartoon, as a cold pit grew in his stomach.

How had anybody known? He was sure nobody had seen them. No, he knew nobody had seen them. Perhaps they hadn't been as careful as they should have been, but he was convinced they'd been lucky.

"It's awful, isn't it? Although you look good—much better than Harrington did. You at least look proud, not like you've never had a thought above your waistline."

He kept staring at the picture—at the drawing of himself and Linnette. As with the other cartoon, she stood in the fore-ground, her belly huge and pregnant—very different from the lush but slender curves of her true frame. He stood behind, one arm wrapped around her, his hand splayed upon that full belly. She was right, he did look proud. How would he look if she were in truth growing his child? Could she be? It might just be possible.

He lifted his head and stared at her pale face. "Do we need to talk about this?"

Linnette caught his meaning quickly as she watched his eyes drop to her belly and then back to her face. He might only have been back from Canada for a few weeks, but she'd always un-derstood the way he thought—sometimes too well. Had he not been listening? She was tempted to speak in single, well-spaced syllables. "How many times must I say it? I am *not* with child. There is nothing to talk about." And oh how she wished that were true.

Before James had returned, her life had been simple, but now it was anything but. She spent her days and her nights longing for James, for the uncontrollable passion—and peace—she found in his arms, in those few stolen hours that they managed to be alone. But those hours were so few—and could never be more. They shouldn't exist at all. Nobody would ever understand their relationship, understand how the ever-proper dowager duchess had ended up leaning against a tree, her skirts about her waist within minutes of meeting the man again, everything abandoned to the flare of passion that had always consumed them. Even now, bristling with anger, she could feel her desires rise as she watched his long fingers tap against his leg, drawing her gaze. She pressed her legs tight together and folded her hands in her skirts, resisting the urge to reach out and stroke him—or hit him. Her emotions were never rational when he was about.

James took a step nearer to her, the muscles of his thighs showing firm beneath his tight trousers.

She swallowed, unable to draw her eyes from those power-ful legs, from thoughts of them lying beneath her.

"I must disagree. There are certainly still things to talk about," he said. "Assuming you were with child, would it be mine?"

Her head snapped up. "You, you, you . . ." She began sput-tering, her pent-up emotions let loose by his audacity. How dare he! He might have only been in her life for a few weeks, but who else did he think was a possibility? Was there any-thing she could throw? Her gaze darted about the parlor. If only they were someplace else. He was certainly not worth any of her carefully collected treasures.

And there was no baby. That was the most certain thing of all. Whoever had created the drawing was seeking a scandal, nothing more.

She closed her eyes, turned away from the temptation of staring at him, at his broad shoulders and understanding eyes, at his easy acceptance of all life would throw at him and his ability to manage it. Perhaps sending for him had not been wise. Experience had taught her better than to think she could depend upon him.

"And who else do you imagine could be the mythical father of my mythical child? Do you have any suggestions?"

James walked across the room and sat on the corner of a sturdy Tudor table, his long legs spread before him. "Well, the first cartoon placed you with the Duke of Harrington. He seems like a reasonable guess—even if you've already said otherwise, and I do believe you."

"I am glad, given that I have not been with the man in years." As she spoke, she questioned herself. Did she mean for her words to wound him, as he had once wounded her? Is that why she had laid bare her past affair? Did she sound like a witch? Did she mean to make him jealous? "We were together only twice—soon after my husband died. It would have to be the longest pregnancy in history."

James's face had stilled at her words, his thoughts unreadable. He turned away. "What about my distant cousin and heir presumptive, Mr. Swatts? I believe he calls on you frequently." Staring up at the portrait of her husband's mother over the mantel, he looked like he was actually contemplating the question. "His conversation has suggested a close relationship with you."

"It has? I'd sooner sleep with my horse. The only reason he came calling at all was that he kept hoping you would not be found alive and he wanted information from me. I've never seen a man so eager for a title. He could barely hide his delight when rumors surfaced that you might have died in battle." She swallowed, fighting to hide how she had felt upon hearing those same rumors. "He still stops by and tries to wheedle any new information from me. He is determined to charm all my secrets from me, although he's about as charming as that one-eyed stable cat that always has a rat's tail between its teeth. I have as little to do with the man as possible."

"Ouch. You should not abuse the poor man in such a fashion. He is my cousin, you know." He crossed one ankle over the other, again drawing her gaze to his long legs—and higher.

Even wanting to strangle him, it was all she could do not to step toward him, to press her breasts to his chest, to hold his head tight between her hands, fingers locked in silky hair, as she plundered those hard lips with all the skill she had. Instead, she lifted her gaze to his face, meeting his steady stare. "And you dislike him even more than I do. You must know he is plotting to prove that you should not have inherited the title."

"I suppose, then, that I will have to believe that he could not have fathered your child. He would not want to risk another potential claimant."

Damn him—and she wasn't even quite sure which "him" she meant. "There—is—no—child. Until you arrived in town I had not been alone with a man in months, perhaps a full year. Unless you think I am carrying on with a footman. Perhaps you think that as I came to your bed with such speed that I carry on this way with everyone." Even as she spoke the words, she realized that she did fear he thought such a thing, that he believed she acted like this with every man.

"That is always possible, I suppose. And it has never been my bed you've come to."

She knew he meant it as a joke, but still . . . If he wasn't careful she was going to kill him someday—although she might be sorry afterwards. She did not want him dead, just gone from here, gone from her life, from her dreams and desires. But none of those seemed possible—and in truth, she was not even sure that was what she wanted.

"Are you trying to make me hit you with something?" she asked, her breath increasing with the effort to feign calm. "You know this whole conversation is preposterous. I am not with child and therefore there is no father."

He stood again and stretched, his hands reaching toward the high ceiling. The man really was huge. It was one of the things she'd always adored about him. She was not a small woman, and yet next to him she felt petite and dainty. She should not be thinking such things, much less acting on them. She needed to leave London and soon. The blasted man was a most addicting drug. It would be hard to leave him, to be without him for a second time, but she knew things could not continue as they were.

She took a step nearer, pulled by invisible powers that held them both, her mind full of all the things she wished could be. His gaze met hers and the pull grew stronger. His eyes dropped to the pale flesh of her bosom above the fabric of her dress and she felt her breasts grow heavy with longing, with the desire for his touch. His eyes rose again and her breath caught at the naked longing they held.

It was an endless second of want, of need.

Then he turned away and strode to the window, his arms at ease by his sides, pretending that nothing had happened, that the second had not existed. "How can you be so sure you are not with child? After these last weeks we have spent together I'd think there would be some possibility."

Blast. Leave it to James to come to the heart of the matter. How could he speak sense when her entire being ached for his touch? God, she wished she could go back in time and erase that first night of his return, erase the joy at seeing him after so long, erase the foolish way her heart had sped, the desire that had filled her, the thought that she was being given one last chance at true happiness. If she could erase that then she could erase all that had happened since then—erase her inability to stay away from him. It had all been a dream—a dream she needed to wake from.

She forced her brain to reason, her voice to normalcy. "I would have to admit that perhaps it is possible, but it is highly unlikely. I know my body well—those courses you were speaking of—and it is not likely that I would have conceived a child during this stretch of time. And in any case, if I were pregnant, it would be months before I looked anything like I do in these prints."

Turning her desire to anger, she stalked over to the table and lifted the sheet of paper he had left behind. She spread it open and stared down—and felt her mood shift yet again. Her huge pregnant belly seemed to fill the whole page—or at least it did in her mind. What would it be like to be pregnant? To actually carry his child? One hand wanted to move toward her stomach, but she held it back. The gesture could easily be misinterpreted.

She studied the line drawing, looking past her sudden longing.

James looked fine. The eight years he'd been away had actually improved his looks, moving him from boyhood charm to a man's hard angles—and muscles. She, however, looked like a melon with witchy eyes and straggly black hair.

She ripped the paper in half, crumpled it, and almost threw it in the empty fireplace, wishing there were flames so that she could watch it burn to ash. There were not, however, and she wasn't sure she wished to leave the evidence of her upset and anger for the servants to find.

Not that it mattered much when half the shop windows in London were likely to have it pasted to them. These devilish cartoons had already cost her her best friend. Kathryn, the Duchess of Harrington, had not spoken to her since the last one had appeared, the one of Linnette and Kathryn's husband—not that it had helped that Linnette had been forced to confess an affair with Harrington far in the past.

Damnation. How could one drawing incite so much trouble?

And who had even thought up the blasted thing? Nobody knew about her and James. Nobody.

Well, that was not quite true.

Elizabeth had seen that first kiss, had seen how quickly fire could ignite. Linnette didn't want to think it could be Elizabeth, surely even she would not have . . . Their friendship had always been difficult, but Linnette still considered Elizabeth a friend.

Linnette lifted her face and tilted her head to consider

James as he stood staring out her parlor window—no, his parlor window. She must begin to remember that this was all his, or at least near enough so it made no difference. If nothing else, the print made clear that things must change between them.

"You're staring," he said, turning toward her. "Do I have jam on my chin? Would you like to lick it off?"

He didn't, of course. He only meant to tease her, to lighten the heavy mood that lay between them—but the images that filled her mind made her wish very much that he did. Her fingers clenched. The paper crunched. She looked down at the print, wished she'd thrown it on the hearth, wished she could just ignore it completely. But she could not.

She stepped away, deliberately turning her back to James, to the continued shift of emotion between them.

"I wish the world were different," she said with a weariness she had not realized she felt.

She heard his steps behind her and then a prickle of shock as he laid a hand on her shoulder, his thumb brushing the nape of her neck. She should have shaken him off, drawn away, but it felt so good. She longed to lean back against him, to let his touches, his kisses, his passions, take her away from this place, back to the past, to the distant past when she'd still had belief—and hope.

She crushed the print in her hand again and then held up her fist, the bits of crumpled paper visible between her fingers. "This could ruin me, ruin both of us."

"It's only nonsense." James closed his large hand about her fist, hiding the remnants of the cartoon from view. "Nobody cares. I certainly don't. What does it matter if the world knows about us? I've never thought much of society and see no reason to start now."

"Nobody cares? Not even you can be that naive. You've been too many years in the wilds. The whole world will care."

"Why on earth should they?" He trailed his thumb across her neck again. "And why do we care if they do?"

Linnette let herself go for one brief second, relaxing against him, and then grabbed for her strength, for the rationality she should never have relinquished, and turned to face him full on. She could not help the bitterness that seeped into her voice. "Not care that the Dowager Duchess of Doveshire is sleeping with, having sex with—indeed fucking, James Sharpeton, the new Duke of Doveshire? The Dowager and the new Duke. It sounds like a Minerva Press novel. I think they will care very much. Nobody will care that you were only distantly related to my husband or that we grew up together. Instead every strata of society will be talking of how I am trying to manipulate you or how you are taking advantage of me. And among the ton, among my friends, my acquaintances, I imagine the gossip will be of nothing else. Everyone knows I've run the dukedom for years and enjoyed doing so, fought to do so. Now they will all be saying that I seduced you to keep my power, that I am doing everything I can to control the one man who will take it all away from me."

Chapter Two

"I've never had any intention of taking what is yours, Linnette." James had not once guessed that she thought that way, but he could feel her own fear as she spoke of what others would say. She'd always seemed so confident, so sure. Even now, Linnette projected anger over the print, not worry or despair. It was only because he understood her so well that he could see more, could see the full range of emotion that held her from moment to moment. "I could not have been more stunned than when I found out I was the new duke. I've told you I never imagined, much less wanted such a thing."

"That does not change the fact that you are the duke—and that you are home, returned." Linnette spoke with quiet dignity, her face but inches from his own, her body held close by his continued grasp on her fist, by his hand against her neck. Her sweet breath brushed his cheek. "Even in these last few weeks, since everyone has known of your arrival, I have felt the difference. I may have been the dowager duchess for several years, but only now do I feel it. I always considered it a lark—I certainly never felt a dowager—until you arrived and turned my world upside down, leaving me no purpose."

"I know we have not talked of it—perhaps we should have, but my days have been so busy with learning to understand my new role in life. You have never mentioned that you were not happy with the change in affairs. I had imagined you were relieved to see the last of the account books, to have somebody else take the responsibility. And as we have discussed, I will still need a hostess—and despite this—," he squeezed her fingers about the cartoon, "—and what lies between us, I see no reason that you cannot fulfill the role. I understand that you throw a magnificent party and you've certainly managed my houses smoothly."

"But that's just it. They are your houses now. Perhaps I should have said something earlier, but there has never been a good time. When we are alone we—we are always occupied with things other than talk." She said it flatly, but her eyes spoke of memories. "And when we are in company it would hardly be appropriate. Women do not run estates if there are men about. I have always known that there would be a new duke and that my position would change. But if you think that I would be happy managing your houses and arranging balls— all the while waiting for you to marry and for your wife to come and usurp my role, you have not been paying attention. Is that really the type of woman you think I am?"

God, how did a man begin to answer that?

"First of all, I have no intention of marrying any time in the near future—or even the not-so-near future. Until I inherited I hadn't thought to marry at all." Not since he'd left her, but he did not say that. "And as for what type of woman you are— how should I know after all these years? You are correct that our time alone has not been spent in discussion. All I know at present is that you pour tea with elegance, know the names of every single servant I employ, have apparently decorated my homes in a style that is fashionable but still allows a man to relax—and that you still gasp my name when you climax." He knew he should not have added that last, but sometimes he needed to provoke her, to find out what she really felt, really thought. It was clear they had not spent enough time in honest discussion. "That hardly seems enough to define you. The girl I knew would have been quite happy managing my home and raising my children. You used to say it was all you wanted, all you dreamed of. Has that changed?"

She paled at his words, appearing wounded rather than angry, tried to step away, but his hand still tight about her fist held her in place. "Well, if you had not spent the last eight years in Canada maybe you'd know more than how I cry your name in passion. Not that I believe that you care. Why did you stay away for so long, James?" She tilted her chin up and glared, asking the question he had avoided for two long weeks.

"So finally we come to that."

Why *had* he stayed away? Now, when he was close to her, when he felt her body so near to his own it was inconceivable that he had not come running the moment he was able. He had never wanted anything as much as he wanted her. It had never mattered that it was impossible—that the world stood between them—so why had he stayed away?

He shut his eyes, blocking her questioning eyes from his view and tried to find rational thought. For those first years away he'd been in the Army and he'd had no choice—and then there had been her marriage. How could he have returned when she had been married to another? Even worse, to his distant cousin?

The knowledge alone had been a form of torture.

But why had he not come back after that? Why had he not come back when he heard Doveshire had died?

He opened his eyes and stared down at her, trying to find the answer he had so long avoided. It was hard to meet her gaze and he dropped his glance lower. The yellow she wore this morning was a far quieter color than she normally chose. It was a simple gown with lacings in the front. He'd never seen a woman of her position clothed in such a dress. It was more something that a maid or farmwife would have worn.

Still, he liked it. It showed off her breasts to perfection— and he was so close to her—it would be so easy to unfasten, to open, to slide back and . . . Damn, his body continued to respond. He needed to be thinking with his head not his—. But despite his best intentions he found himself reaching, his hand gliding down the brushed velvet skin of her shoulder.

"Stop." She stepped as far back as his hold would allow. "Are you going to answer me? Every time we try to talk we become distracted. I want an answer." Her gaze followed the small gesture of his fingers, which still moved as if stroking her skin—and he did not miss the darkening of her eyes or the quickening of her breath.

There was some temptation to distract her further, to give in to what they both were feeling, to pull her to the settee and to make sure that no further words left her lips for at least an hour—he knew that he could, that she would not stand strong for long. He took a half-step forward, let their bodies brush, and then released her hand, turning away and walking back to the window.

"Well?" She was persistent.

"Why did I not return earlier? Well, you were married, if I recall." He fingered the lace curtains.

"Doveshire died four years ago."

He waited for her to say more, but she evidently felt that was response enough, forcing him to find the next words. "I liked Canada, the endless wilds, the rich forests, the immense possibilities. A man can be whatever he wants in a land like that."

"That is no answer. You could have been whatever you wanted here—and you could have had me."

It sounded so simple when she phrased it like that. "You were already engaged to Doveshire when I left. That does not sound like I could have had you."

"I became engaged to Doveshire when I was five-years-old. I hardly think that counts. I would never have married him if you had stayed."

He could feel her green gaze burning holes in his back. "I know." He swept a hand through his hair.

"You *know*? You know and you left anyway?" He thought he heard her choke back a sound, but after a moment she continued in a voice full of deadly control. "If you won't tell me why you didn't come back after Doveshire's death, can you at least tell me why you left? One day I slept in your arms in my mother's summer cottage and the next all I had was a note saying you'd decided to take up a commission and were off to the Americas. I didn't even know it could happen so fast. I thought those things took time."

"I never will get used to hearing you refer to Doveshire's death while everybody around me calls me by the same title. I think I am drawn to you as much because you call me by my name, call me James, as for any other reason. I will never feel like Doveshire."

She didn't answer for a moment. He knew she wondered if his thought was sincere or merely an effort to change the subject. Then she spoke, her words carefully chosen. "I suppose it must be strange for you. Given that you are the fourth Doveshire I've known, it does not seem so odd to me. And it never seemed odd to Charles, to my husband—as well you know. He grew up knowing he was going to be duke after his father. I think he simply took it as his due."

That was certainly true. Even as a lad Charles had acted like he was duke already. And he had hated to be called Charles, always wanting to be referred to by his courtesy title, Mithawk. "And my immediate predecessor, my unfortunate distant cousin, how did he manage the change?" he asked, turning to sit on the wide windowsill, leaning back against its framing.

"I never actually met him," Linnette answered. "He kept delaying his return from India and then—well, you know the story—his ship sank and he died along with his entire family, including all three of his sons."

"I was more sorry than you can imagine when I heard of it." He looked down at his hands, folded in his lap. It was hard to hold still, he wanted to pace, to run, to fuck, to work his body until his mind was empty of her questions.

"In any case . . ." She coughed a little, and he could almost hear her shaking her head to clear it. "I never knew how he felt about becoming the duke. It is hard to catch those nuances in correspondence. I suppose he must have felt strange about it. It was quite unexpected when he inherited. He was the son of my husband's youngest uncle. It was never thought that he would inherit. Everybody always imagined that Charles and I would . . ."

". . . that you would have children. You can say it. I expected it also. It was so unlike Charles to catch a fever and be dead three days later. When I was a boy he seemed invincible."

"Yes, I know. I felt the same." Her soft footsteps moved closer, until he could see the tips of her slippers.

They were a bright pink. Despite everything, it was enough to make him smile. With hair the color of a copper penny Linnette had never been able to wear pink. He could remember her crying about it as a girl. She must have decided that her feet were far enough from her hair to make the color allowable.

"Don't think I haven't noticed how carefully you changed the subject. I still want to know both why you left England and why you didn't want to return. Why did you leave me alone for so long after Charles died? If you had come back then, perhaps we could truly have been together—it would have not have seemed so odd. You would not yet have been duke and we could have gone away, quietly." She took another step toward him, clearly demanding an answer.

"From what I hear you weren't always alone. You mentioned Harrington." He wished he could call back the words the moment they escaped his lips. He kept his eyes focused on those raspberry slippers.

She stepped back, as if slapped. "That was uncalled for. Do you claim there were no other women the whole time you were away? I would be quite sure that they numbered—numbered far greater than the men I—I kept company with."

He lifted his head, finally, and stared into her large, green eyes. "I am sure you are correct, Linnette. I have never claimed to be a saint. It is quite unfair that I would expect differently of you."

"I wish that I could say there had only been you, James." Her voice was so quiet he could barely hear it. "When I first gave myself to you I was sure I would never have another lover. You were my one and only—my always."

"And then I left."

"Yes. Then you left me."

Could he tell her why he had gone? That, he did know the answer to. The need for secrecy was long past. Still, was there any purpose in it? It would only hurt her, make her feel betrayed by those she trusted.

"Did your parents ever speak to you about my leaving?" he asked.

"No, not that I recall—at least not beyond stating it as a matter of fact. My mother was far too busy planning my coming out and then my betrothal ball to have thoughts of anything else."

"And your father?"

"No." She looked thoughtful a moment. "Although there was a day a few months after you left, just before my actual coming out, that he pulled me aside and asked me if I needed to contact you. I never did understand why."

James understood all too well. Her father had been well aware of the physical nature of their relationship and had certainly been trying to determine if he'd left behind any unwelcome gifts. He was surprised that Linnette had not understood the conversation—if not then, later. She was not a naive or innocent woman any longer.

"Why are you asking me all these questions? What do my parents have to do with your leaving?"

Had she truly never understood that either? He would have thought it the most logical of answers. It was part of why he had followed her father's directions and left such a simple note. He had always imagined that she would figure it out on her own.

Did she not understand how much her father had wanted her to become a duchess?

"Oh, what does it matter now?" He said it as a simple fact, with not a trace of avoidance or anger in his voice. "Why do we not go back to what caused this whole mess?" He strode around her and picked up the crumpled paper she'd left sitting on the table.

He smoothed out the pieces, fitting the halves together.

"What do we do about this?" he asked.

He was avoiding her questions—as he always did. No, that was unfair. He had not avoided them these past weeks because she had not asked. She, too, had been happy to deal only with the day-to-day details needed to help him take over the estates, happy to let all else get smothered in the heat of their passion.

Oh, she had not asked because she too had been content to live only in the present or in the distant past of their joint childhood—the years in between off limits—they had both been afraid of the answers to these questions.

Suppressing a sigh, Linnette walked over and stared down at the torn sheet of paper. She'd spent so many years being respectable. It was true that she'd had some discreet fun as well, but it had always been discreet. There was not a home in all of Mayfair that was not open to her.

And now this.

Two cartoons in just over a week—and this second one she deserved.

Two cartoons that seemed to have no purpose save to ruin her life.

She laid her hand on the paper, smoothing it further. Elizabeth. She still did not want to think her long-time friend could be behind this, but who else could it be? She knew Elizabeth believed she had deliberately stolen James from her—although she could not understand the logic behind the thought. Yes, Elizabeth had said she felt ready to take a lover. Yes, Elizabeth had indicated that the new duke just might do. But none of that made James hers—even if she hadn't known of Linnette's past with James. And Linnette certainly could not help what had happened between her and James—if she could have she most certainly would have. She did not like feeling she had so little control.

She shook her head to clear it. Such thought was unproductive.

Lifting her eyes, she met James's topaz gaze. "I don't know what to do. I suppose that is why I am so angry. Denial will only bring more talk."

"That does seem to be the same the world over."

She stepped further away. There really was only one answer.

It was the one that she had been considering all morning, the one she wanted. So why was it so hard to say the words? "The best answer may be for us to stay apart. It is time for you to move into this house. It is the duke's residence. You have lodged at the hotel long enough."

"That, I will agree with. It does seem reasonable for me to move in. If I am going to be the duke, I should start living as one."

"And I will move out. Perhaps I will return to Dovecroft Court and begin to move my belongings to the dower house. If I leave during the season, it will be very clear there is nothing between us."

"You cannot leave." He stepped forward, following her, his presence fanning the flames she was fighting to keep banked. "If you leave Town, everyone will wonder if you are hiding."

"Perhaps, but it is the best solution. I will have to be seen again in a few months so that all can see my waistline is still slender—or perhaps I'll invite guests to come to the country with me. I'll choose a gossiping old biddy and then everyone will know that there was nothing to the cartoon."

"You can't leave." He moved again, gaze locked on her, his eyes telling a story all their own.

She held her ground. "It is the most sensible thing. I certainly cannot stay in this house with you. That would be beyond adding fuel to the fire. It would be adding gunpowder."

He took one more step, but then stopped. "I don't care—and neither should you. We will know the truth."

"And the truth will be that they are all correct. We were lovers—we have sex—frequently."

"So?"

"Don't pretend you don't understand. You may have lived in the wilds for years, but you were not raised by wolves."

"No, I was raised by my stepfather, a vicar who never looked beyond the walls of his library, and my older sister, who has never once been ten miles from the town where she was born. I think wolves might have cared more about society." He was glaring at her now, the muscles in his cheek clenched tight.

Her own temper rose again in response, her whole body readying for the fight. She felt the heat growing within her, demanding a release, any release. At least with a fight she felt some control, some power. "You still know exactly what I mean."

"You are right. I do know. I just do not care. Why be a duke if I can't bloody well do what I want?"

Had he grown taller? It certainly seemed that way.

Linnette would not be cowed. She tilted her chin up and narrowed her eyes. "What do you bloody want?"

His eyes dropped to her breasts, which she could feel heaving against her simple gown.

"Besides that?" she said, forcing her voice to remain quiet.

"What if I just want you and I don't care who knows it?" He stepped even closer, the buttons of his shirt almost brushing against her.

"You've already had me—and left me. I promise that I am not worth the scandal." Her breath caused the loops of his cravat to ripple.

"And if I think you are? That we are?"

"Then what are you proposing—marriage? Should I take

this as a true proposal? Last time you got down on bended knee."

She could feel the breath leave him.

"And if I am?"

And then it happened—she did not mean it to—she tried to suppress it—but still it came. Laughter bubbled up out of her, hard, frantic, uncontrollable laughter that cost too much to be suppressed and hurt too much to be stopped.

She could not control it, could not breath through the feelings that bubbled from within. The force of emotions that had been held in check for the morning, for the last weeks, for the eight years since he left, all took hold of her at once, bending her forward, tears leaking from the corners of her eyes. "Me, marry you?"

CHAPTER THREE

She was laughing at him. He'd proposed, something he'd done but once before in his entire life, and she laughed—she actually giggled and tittered—and something else that sounded rather like the braying of a donkey.

She was laughing at him.

He'd never stood much on masculine pride, but hurt and anger were rapidly replacing what little control he had left. The pain and desire of nearly a decade coalesced in a single moment.

He grabbed her shoulders, pulled her forward, pressing her breasts tight against his chest.

He stared down at her—at the laughter still tumbling from her.

And he kissed her, giving in to the desire that had been plaguing him all morning, that inability to keep his hands off her.

What else was a man to do?

His lips met hers, hard, determined, engulfing. Holding her even tighter he ground his mouth down upon hers. This was for him. She was his and it was bloody well time she knew it.

Her hands came up, pressing upon his chest, scratching his neck, and he didn't care.

Better a lioness, a hellcat, than a laughing shrew.

She bit him.

He nipped back, catching her lush lower lip between his teeth and exerting just enough pressure to hold her captive.

Oh, she was not laughing now.

She twisted, trying to catch his lip. He held her back. He was the master now. This time it was not a game. She was his.

Her shoulders pulled back, her knee came up—he pulled her tighter. Then slid his arms lower, settled them about her well-rounded ass and lifted her off her feet, drawing her legs about his hips, settling her just where he wanted her.

She bit at him again. He tasted blood. Hers? His? It did not matter.

He slid his tongue into her mouth, daring her to bite him harder.

Her head pulled back again, but only enough that she could stare into his eyes. He could see passions of all kinds kindled there.

And then flames took over both of them.

Lips pressed to lips, tongues danced.

His neckwear was gone. Her dress gaped open, tempting him.

He tore his mouth from hers, and bent awkwardly, burying his face there, in her breasts, thinking he could die in this moment and not regret it.

Damn, her dress was still too tight. He wanted to work it free, but his hands were well filled with squirming, wiggling woman, woman pressing tight exactly where he wanted to be pressed. He thrust his hips forward and felt the response run through her. He thrust again.

The table. That heavy table that had held his weight without a creak.

He turned, settling her upon it. Her legs were still tight about his hips and he leaned forward just enough to secure her to the surface. One of his hands slipped forward, pulled at the lacings of her dress until all was bare before him.

Her nipples stood proud, her full breasts rising and falling with speed. What more could a man want, need?

He bent, catching one of those darkened peaks between his teeth, and then drew it deep into his mouth, feasting, devouring, claiming.

She was his. He hoped he marked her, hoped that his claim would be as visible as it was real.

Panting, her head thrown back, she lay spread before him. It was a matter of seconds to push her skirts high, to unfasten the fall of his pants—one further thrust—and heaven. She was so ready for him, her hot, wet body closing about him, drawing him in. Nothing had ever felt so good, so needed.

He moved, back and forth, fast and slow, enjoying the sounds of their bodies, the sigh of lips, the slap of flesh.

Harder and harder.

He opened eyes he had not realized he had closed and found her staring up at him, her eyes almost black with want. She braced her arms behind her and thrust up with her hips— driving him for her own pleasure, her own desires.

And then she tensed, her head thrown back again even as her body lifted—and clenched, and clenched again. She was biting her own lips, hard, in an attempt not to cry out.

That would not do. He ground harder, added the twist that he knew she could not resist—and listened as his name echoed through the room.

And then it was all about him. He closed his eyes and let everything go but sensation.

Again and again he moved—blocking out all but his pleasure, the driving need.

And then it came—the world spreading and then tightening to that one pinpoint before it all burst free.

He felt her name rise within him, but he held it back—not now—not—

A last single burst—and then collapse.

He lay upon her, his chest heaving with the desire for air. The soft breeze of her breaths blew across him, cooling him.

He drew himself up, stared down at her as she lay more beautiful than he'd ever seen her—her passion spent, only softness remaining.

He wanted to ask again—but masculine pride would not allow it.

Laughter echoed through his mind.

Bloody hell.

He quickly fastened himself up, pulled off his ruined cravat, stuffed it in a pocket—and turned away.

He did not look back until he'd slammed the door behind him.

He was gone. Linnette knew it before his weight left her, before he stayed silent, before the door slammed behind him.

Her laughter had brought them to this, to the mindless release of the passion that lay between them.

And she had nothing to say. How could she call back words she had not said? How could she make him listen to words he would not want to hear?

She'd agreed to marry him once—almost nine years ago.

She'd let her heart fill with joy until it almost burst within her chest.

She'd let her world be perfect—and then he'd left.

Left with only a few words scribbled on a piece of paper— left without a care or a thought.

She'd said "yes" once. She never would again.

The cost was just too high.

She slid down the table until her feet found purchase on the floor. She shook out her skirts, while trying to shake sense into herself. She'd done the right thing. It might have been unintentional, but she'd sent James away. She hadn't meant to hurt him in the process, but perhaps there had been no other way.

She shoved her breasts into place, rapidly refastening her laces. She'd put on this gown this morning simply because it was fast and comfortable and she'd been unable to bear stillness. Now, she could only be glad she did not require help. James had certainly not bothered to wait and see if she did.

A tear formed at the corner of her eye and she brushed it away, wishing she could pretend that it was left over from her mindless laughter. It was not.

James always waited to see if she needed help. He brought her damp cloths and wiped her clean. He lay sweet kisses upon her back as he fastened her up or—on those few occasions that he'd slipped in after dark—he smoothed her pillows and shook the sheets to grant her a comfortable night's sleep.

He always showed her every care and consideration.

Not this time.

This time she could have been a dockside doxy for all the attention he showed.

Another tear. This one slipping down her cheek before she could stop it.

This was what she wanted, what she needed.

She could not have him, therefore she must be free of him.

She would have the maids pack her things and then leave. Leave James to this grand house and—and to everything. Her whole life was here—and now she didn't know what she had.

She sniveled.

And that was enough to stop her.

She was Linnette Sharpeton, the Dowager Duchess of Doveshire.

She did not snivel and certainly not over a man.

Yes, she would go to the country and retire for a while, but she would not do it with undo haste or hurry. A few more days in Town would help ensure that nobody paid any attention to these vile comics. She would walk in the park, buy herself a new ball gown—as slimly cut as fashion would allow—and she would show them all that nothing had changed.

Nothing.

And . . .

She shook her skirts one more time and strode over to the table where the torn paper still lay. Grabbing it with one hand she once again scrunched it into a tight ball and then tucked it into her sleeve. She would burn it later. Perhaps she'd even find a witch's spell to recite.

Elizabeth would pay. Her emotion, her anger might be misplaced—even in this state she recognized that—but it did not matter. Nobody, not even the Countess of Westhampton, would be allowed to play with Linnette's life in this fashion.

"Lady Westhampton and Lady Richard Tennant wish an audience, your grace. They are waiting in the hall. Should I show them to the parlor or tell them you are not receiving?"

James started at the sound of his porter's voice. He'd been sitting here in his office, in his house, trying to decide what to do—and waiting for her. Where the hell was she? He'd come back to the house ready to—

He wasn't quite sure what he was ready to do. Apologize? It would be easiest, but he wasn't convinced he was at fault.

He had behaved badly, very badly, but so had she. She'd laughed. His belly tensed at the thought.

Still, something had to be done, had to be said.

He'd been tempted to avoid her, but she did live in his house, still helped manage his estates, and there was no way he could stay away. Not that he was sure he could have stayed away from her anyway.

A soft cough from the door.

He looked up, glanced back at the porter.

"Who?" He knew exactly who they were, of course. Or at least, he knew exactly who Lady Westhampton was. He had been introduced to her a few times and she'd made herself known to him on several more occasions over the last weeks.

If he hadn't already been involved with Linnette, he might even have been interested in pursuing her. She had exotic good looks, reminiscent of an Indian princess, and he'd met a few.

But he was involved with Linnette, to his great satisfaction despite their—their disagreement this morning, and so had no interest in any other woman. As a result, he actually found Lady Westhampton annoying.

"Lady Westhampton and Lady Richard Tennant," the porter repeated, managing to keep a straight face while giving the impression that he thought James might be a trifle batty.

What on earth could they want? "Just send them in. Are you sure they wish to see me and not her grace? I believe she is out at present but will perhaps be returning shortly." Did he sound too hopeful?

"They asked for you, your grace."

Leaning back in his chair, James stared blankly down at his desk and tried to center his mind on his guests. It was unusual to receive female callers. Ladies always expected the gentlemen to call on them. He understood it was much more respectable that way.

A moment later there was the patter of slippers and the rustle of silk skirts and the ladies arrived.

He stood. "Welcome to my home, ladies. And how may I be of service to you?" He gestured for them to be seated, and then returned to his own chair.

Lady Westhampton immediately shot him a look from under her lashes as if the idea of "being of service" had many connotations. Her lips curved with good humor.

"We've come to ask you a great favor," the other lady, a quiet, but pretty, brunette, began.

She must be Lady Richard. She was looking at him as if they were acquainted, so they must have been introduced at some function over the last weeks. She must be one of Linnette's friends. He didn't remember her, but given the number of introductions he'd suffered through, and his current state of mind, that was not surprising. "I could never refuse a favor to such gracious ladies."

Was that overdoing it? His social skills were rusty after his time in Canada and he'd yet to find the right balance of flattery and fact.

"Not refuse a favor—that is good to know. And you must call me, Elizabeth. I know it is most improper, but we will hopefully be working quite closely together," Lady Westhampton added, an edge of innuendo lurking in her tone.

"And you may call me, Annie." Lady Richard shot a look at her friend. She was clearly not happy with the suggestion. "We are here on serious business, on charitable business."

"Yes?"

"As you may know, Doveshire has long supported the Orphanage of Lost Angels," Annie began. "Lady Westhampton, Elizabeth, and I are on the board of directors, along with being patronesses ourselves, and wish to be sure you plan on continuing Doveshire's support. It would be most dreadful for the poor children if you did not."

Orphans? He was supporting orphans? Or perhaps it was simpler to say that Doveshire was. James had not quite become accustomed to thinking of himself as a whole dukedom. "If Doveshire has always supported such an undertaking I would imagine that I will continue to do so." There, that did not commit him before he'd had a chance to look into the institution, but also left everyone contented for the moment.

"I am pleased to hear it." Elizabeth gave him a very direct look, a look that told him just how she'd like to be pleased. Leaning forward, she gifted him with a view well below the neckline of her dress. He swallowed and tried to look away without being obvious. Why had the woman decided to target him?

"And will you continue to host the meetings? We've found your house a most convenient location for our board meetings, your grace." Annie smiled at him with true sweetness.

"I am sure you should speak to the dowager duchess about that, Annie," he answered. "I would assume that it was she who made all such arrangements in the past." Where was Linnette? She should be home by now. Surely the staff would have told him if she'd actually left, gone to the country, wouldn't they? "I am hoping that she will agree to act as my hostess in the future."

There was a moment of silence. The two women looked at each other and he could sense a sudden awkwardness.

"Yes, her grace hosted all of our meetings in the past," Annie answered, but did not meet his gaze.

"Then I am sure that she will be happy to do so in the future." James could not help but wonder why the women suddenly refused to look at him. Even Elizabeth seemed to have lost her boldness.

"There may be some difficulty with that." It was Annie who spoke again. "I do not know if you are aware that the orphanage is supported by both parishes in Doveshire and in Harrington."

"And?" He wished that they would just cut to the heart of the matter.

"The Duchess of Harrington, Kathryn, and Linnette traditionally arranged things between them," Annie answered after another pause. "We are at a bit of a loss without their leadership. We were hoping that perhaps you could speak to the dowager duchess."

"I am still not sure that I understand the problem." And he wasn't sure he was the one to speak with Linnette—at least not at this moment.

Elizabeth finally lifted her head and met his gaze. "I do not know if you are aware of certain—certain drawings that have been circulating in the past weeks."

Ahh, it began to make sense. "Yes, I believe that I know what you refer to."

"Kathryn and Linnette are simply not speaking. It makes everything quite complicated," Annie said.

"And so you wish me to become involved. Would it not be simpler for one of you to speak to Linnette yourselves?" He swung one leg over the other and leaned back.

Again, he could sense the tension grow. Annie seemed to have taken a great interest in her hands and Elizabeth no longer gave any appearance of seeking a closer acquaintance.

"I am afraid that the dowager duchess is not fond of either of us at the moment either." Annie stood and moved to stare up at the portrait over the mantel.

"She blames me for the debacle, if you must know." Elizabeth rose from chair and marched toward his desk. "For some reason she believes I am responsible for the cartoon of her and Harrington."

"And are you?" James could not help but ask, his anger from this morning beginning to form again. Whoever was behind the cartoons had much to answer for.

"Certainly not." Elizabeth sounded genuinely affronted. "I would never stoop to such behavior. I am more than capable of letting society know my views without resorting to such low methods."

"That is true," Annie spoke quietly, but he did not miss her words.

"Then why would the dowager duchess believe such a thing?" James asked.

Elizabeth pursed her lips, and for a moment he did not think she would answer. "I suppose because of you," she said at last.

"Because of me?" He would never understand women. He glanced over to Annie and was relieved to see that she looked equally confused.

Turning away from him, Elizabeth lifted her head to stare at the portrait Annie had been examining. He believed it was the one of his great-grandfather, the last duke in his direct line of descent. "I do not believe I will say more. Suffice it to say that I became aware of your—your relationship with the Linnette before this morning's cartoon appeared."

That did not make the matter any clearer, but he sensed that Elizabeth would say no more.

As both women were now standing, James stood himself. "I will admit that Linnette and I are old friends. We spent our childhoods together and are pleased to be reacquainted. Beyond that it is all misunderstanding."

"Oh, I was sure that was the case." Annie moved from the

mantel and chose a seat facing a small settee. "I told you that you must be mistaken." She nodded to Elizabeth. "Linnette would never behave as you suggested. A kiss can mean many things."

"Not the kiss I saw." Elizabeth turned and, pressing her lips tight, glared at her friend.

"But—" Annie began.

Elizabeth turned to him. "I saw you on the terrace at Lady Smythe-Burke's soiree. I would advise that in the future you keep your tongue in your mouth and your hands out of bodices if you wish to convey only friendship."

CHAPTER FOUR

Should she have come? Linnette stared up at the elegant townhouse of the Marquess of Tattingstong and debated. Was it really only a week ago that she'd stood here with Kathryn and laughed? Even the thought caused anxiety to build in her belly—and that wasn't even considering the events of this morning, events she was trying desperately not think about.

Damn those cartoons!

It was easier to blame the cartoon than to blame anybody—except perhaps Elizabeth. Linnette certainly was not in a mood to examine her own faults.

Although perhaps that was why she found herself here, perhaps she needed an outside opinion. She stopped and examined the house, delaying her entry.

Kathryn was right, the marchioness truly did have a way with flowers and color. If only Kathryn were here now. Why had they argued?

Oh, of course she knew why. But why did such a silly thing have to cause such a ruckus?

And it had been silly to sleep with Richard all those years ago. Only she'd needed somebody when Charles had died and—and Richard had been there, lost in his own pain at his friend's death. Kathryn hadn't even met the man yet, so it seemed wrong of her to blame Linnette.

She needed to talk to Kathryn. Kathryn would know the right thing to do, the right thing to say to James, the right way to make him understand how she felt.

Which was why she was here now. If she couldn't speak to Kathryn she needed to talk to somebody, somebody who would just listen and not pry. Praying that at some point Kathryn would forgive her—not that she thought there was anything to forgive—Linnette walked slowly up to the house, lifted the knocker, and let it clang down.

Nothing happened.

She waited.

Nothing. That was odd. It was a prime hour for calling.

Finally the porter appeared and, after giving her the strangest look—had even he seen the cartoons?—led her back to the gardens while Linnette's maid hurried off to the kitchen.

"Oh, I am so glad you've come," Annabelle, the Marchioness of Tattingstong, exclaimed, rising from a wicker chaise that was set in the shade of a tree.

"Forgive my asking, but do you always greet your guests in the garden?" Linnette answered, her worries making her far too forthright.

Annabelle blushed. "That's right. We met in the garden the last time you were here. Well, I don't have many visitors. And I wasn't expecting any today and I do prefer to be out when the weather is nice. I had a few callers the first weeks I was here—curiosity mostly, I believe, but since then almost none."

"I can't imagine why that should be true." Linnette took the chair that Annabelle directed her to. She would think about sunshine and flowers—and Annabelle's problems. That should be enough to fill her mind—for now.

"On our last meeting we agreed to be friends—to use Christian names—and I plan to continue as if that is the case."

"Please do," Linnette answered. Their last meeting had been the occasion of the unfortunate incident with Kathryn and Elizabeth and that evil cartoon. Linnette was more than willing to pretend that whole day had never happened if Annabelle was.

Almost as if reading her mind, Annabelle said, "I know that we cannot forget what happened the last time you were here. I do fear we will need to talk about it, but it does not need to be now. Tell me why you have come. I would like to pretend that it is for the pleasure of my company, but your face tells me that is not the case."

Well, perhaps Annabelle was correct and they could not pretend their last meeting had not happened. Still, Linnette was willing to move the discussion on to her current worries—and maybe she could help Annabelle as well. "Perhaps I will—in a bit, but first perhaps you should explain your lack of visitors. I sense that it is not a situation you care for."

Annabelle lifted her face and stared up at the cloudless sky. "I should call for tea—or do you care for chocolate? I often drank coffee with my father, but it seems not at all the thing for ladies here."

"Tea would be fine." It would be wonderful, in fact. Linnette's hands felt like ice despite the warm weather and the thought of a warm cup to hold between them was heavenly.

Annabelle summoned the maid and then they were alone again—and silent. Neither of them was eager to start.

"I don't know why I don't have visitors." Annabelle, finally, began to speak. "I mean, I do understand that I am American and that I do not always know quite what to do. Growing up in Boston I believed that my mother was bringing me up in the same fashion as any English lady, but now that I am here a year I am constantly reminded of just how different I am, how different the life I have led is."

"I can understand that," Linnette answered. "Although you do not seem particularly different to me. —Still, your speech is . . ."

"A bit odd." Annabelle finished the sentence.

"I was going to say clearly not from London, but then I have cousins from the North who talk with a much stronger accent. You speak with great charm."

"Thank you for saying so. I will pretend to believe you. In any case, I can accept that I was an unexpected addition to society, but I perhaps do not understand why I am such an unwelcome one."

"Well, there are a great many young girls who would have liked to marry a marquess, the heir to a duke, and a great number of mamas who had high hopes. I daresay they may feel you have stolen something that was theirs." Linnette stopped speaking as the maid appeared with tea. The events of the past week had made her unwilling to have even the most casual of conversations overheard.

The maid left and Annabelle poured with grace. She had clearly been practicing. Lifting her glance from the pot, she said, "I suppose I can understand that—but it wasn't like

Thomas, like Tattingstong, was here for them to take. I met him in Boston and he'd already been there well over a decade. He certainly had no intention of returning to London for several years, if ever."

"And then his older brother died and Thomas became a marquess, next in line to a dukedom."

"Yes." Annabelle said the one word, her expression clearly conveying she had no wish to elaborate.

Linnette leaned across the table and patted Annabelle's hand. "I am sure that it is not that you are unwelcome, merely that you are—shall we say—undiscovered. Once you have had more of a chance to mingle in society, then I am sure you will be accepted."

"But how am I to become—discovered if I am rarely invited anywhere and am never called upon?"

"Surely your husband receives invitations?"

"I suppose that he does, but Tattingstong has little interest in attending balls. He seems to have no interest in society."

Linnette sat back and considered, Tattingstong sounded very like James. "I am sure that I and Kathryn can—." She caught herself. It was so easy to forget how quickly friendship could change. "I am sure that I can arrange some invitations for you. And if not, I can—or Doveshire can—host a soiree. I do love arranging a good party."

"Oh would you?" Annabelle's delight was clear.

Linnette swallowed as the thoughts of the morning intruded and her own difficulties coming back to her. "I could, but—."

"Oh, forgive me if I was being presumptuous—if you're having second thoughts, there is no need . . ."

"You misunderstand me." How she could she ask James to host a ball after this morning? She wasn't even sure she ever wished to speak to the man again. "I am only concerned that I may not be able to help, not that I do not wish to. I am afraid that, once I explain why I am here, it will all be too clear."

"I do not understand." Annabelle looked at her with some confusion.

"I am not doing very well at being clear. It is all such a muddle and I don't know where to begin."

"At the beginning?"

Linnette sighed, her mind racing but with no direction. Where was the beginning? Did she even know? "It sounds strange, but I think it actually makes more sense if I begin in the middle. You do remember the cartoon from last week, the one that caused such a mess? The one of me and Harrington?"

The corners of Annabelle's mouth turned up just slightly and she nodded. It was impossible to miss the irony of the situation. "Yes. I must confess I am not sure I'll ever forget. I've never hosted quite such an event."

"You clearly have not been in London long enough. Oh, do forgive me. I am afraid I feel both bitter and brittle this afternoon. I would admit that even in Town it is unusual for one guest to be publicly accused of sleeping with another guest's husband. Privately accused would be another matter. And, of course, it is an almost constant source of gossip. But, yes, the cartoon of me and Kathryn's husband was a trifle extreme."

Wisely, Annabelle said nothing. She nodded just enough to demonstrate her attention.

"That cartoon was a lie. I have not slept with Harrington since long before his marriage. I would never hurt Kathryn in that fashion, even had there been any remaining desire—and as it happens, there is none. Harrington and I are friends and business partners—we spend our time together discussing whether a canal or a railroad could be the best way to get our goods to London. Nothing more."

"I do believe you." And her face said that she did.

"And so, strangely enough, so does everyone else. I was expecting a scandal, but I actually found that everybody believed Harrington was quite happy with Kathryn. And I must admit it doesn't hurt that they've been staring at each other with rapture this whole last week."

"I did see them strolling hand in hand in the park. I didn't even know husbands and wives were allowed to do that," Annabelle commented.

"In any case, other than a few discreet glances at my midline to see if I might be increasing, there had been almost no talk. I was beginning to feel quite relieved."

Annabelle leaned forward, her blond curls falling forward. "I sense a 'but' coming."

"Yes." Linnette pulled her reticule forward and pulled out a copy of the folded cartoon. She'd had to send her maid out to purchase another. Nobody would ever see just how distraught the first copy had made her. "This appeared in shop windows this morning." She unfolded it and spread it on the table.

Annabelle leaned forward and turned the cartoon with a single finger. "Oh dear."

"Yes, 'oh dear,' indeed. People might have believed one cartoon was wrong, but two? I am sure that I'll begin receiving callers bearing knitted baby booties within the day."

"And you're not . . . ?"

"No, I am not." Linnette stood. "Why does everybody ask that? Do I look like I am getting fat?"

"Of course not. But then some women lose weight their first months. And to be honest, these current fashions do not help your cause." Annabelle stood and shook out her dress. "When your skirt expands like a bell from just below your bosom, who knows what is being hidden? I sometimes think I could hide a frigate in here and nobody would know."

Linnette looked down at her own spreading skirts. "I do fear you are correct." She pulled the dress tight. "I have never been slim, but I am certainly not increasing. Perhaps I should try to bring back the fitted waist."

"Or you could throw a grand masquerade and appear in the flimsiest of Grecian drapery."

"Ahh, there is temptation in that." She sat back down in her chair and took a sip of the rapidly cooling tea. "But, I fear you have not quite understood the true problem with the print."

"Oh?" Annabelle sat also.

"I do not like having everyone staring at my belly with a titter, but gossip would soon enough be proved wrong. When I do not ever begin to look like the cartoon, rumor would fade. No, the problem is the man." She stabbed down at the drawing of James.

"Who is he?" Annabelle bent forward to examine the cartoon closely. "He looks familiar. I am sure I've seen him— perhaps even talked to him. He is quite something. A trifle wild looking? Do you even know him?"

"I am afraid that I do. He is James Sharpeton—the new Duke of Doveshire."

Annabelle paused, still staring down, then looked up and met Linnette's gaze. "Ahh, he was on the ship with us from Boston. Although, the cartoon does not do him justice. My father had several long conversations with him and found him good company. And you should have seen his send-off. I think there was a whole regiment wishing him well. They weren't in uniform, of course. Not in Boston. But I do know a military ma—." She stopped midsentence. And Linnette could see understanding spread across her face. "The dowager duchess and the duke. That does sound scandalous—and incestuous—but also just plain silly. I realize that you are quite young—only a year or two older than myself—but I can't imagine you . . ."

"The problem is that I am." The words rushed out. "Oh, I don't believe I just said that. I hadn't actually decided to discuss the matter in detail—and I don't know you at all well—hardly at all—that sounds awful—I just mean that—. Let me just close my mouth for a minute while my brain catches up."

Annabelle lifted the drawing and held it up to her face. "How exactly is he related to your late husband?"

Facts. Linnette could handle answering a question that dealt only with fact. "I am not even sure that I know the correct designation beyond saying they are distant cousins. James and my husband, Charles, shared a great-grandfather. James's grandfather was the third youngest of the four brothers of Charles's grandfather. The title passed directly from father to son for the intervening years until Charles's death."

Even now, four years later, Linnette felt a twinge when she mentioned Charles's death. There was no longer pain, only the ever-continuing sense of disbelief.

Placing the cartoon back on the table, Annabelle clasped her hands in her lap. "I had heard there was quite a search for the new duke. I begin to see why."

"Yes. When James was a boy, he never even considered himself a potential heir. He knew he was Charles's cousin, they joked about it on occasion, but James was always simply the vicar's stepson—bound for the church or the Army. His father had died soon after his birth and his mother never tried to remain close to the duke. They weren't even invited to the more intimate gatherings that the duke, Charles's father, held."

"So you've known the new duke for a while?"

"Since I was a child. One of my father's smaller estates bordered the opposite side of the town from Doveshire's. The vicarage lay between." Linnette felt like she was rambling, but it felt so good to speak of it finally. Her head had been spinning these last weeks since James's return, far before the events of this morning.

"So you all grew up together?"

"My family only stayed there in the summers. My mother found the lake breezes cooling. But, yes, I always felt that I grew up with James. I lived for those months in the summer when I could see him. He was my hero from a very early age."

"And Charles?"

"He was nearly a decade older and always seemed busy." That was simpler than explaining that she'd always known she was betrothed to him and that it had frightened her. And it was the truth. Charles had never shown any interest in her until that last summer.

"So how did you become his wife?"

"Our fathers betrothed us before I reached my fifth birthday. My father's small estate was a finger butting into Doveshire land. The duke wanted it back. My father wanted a great title for his grandchildren. It was a simple exchange."

"There are brief moments when I am glad to be American."

"I do understand—only it would have all gone smoothly. I never felt any true objection to Charles and my father would never have forced me, could not have forced me."

"But . . ."

"I fell in love with James. I wanted to marry James. We had it all planned. I would sell my jewelry and we would buy a small farm and raise horses. It should have been simple. I can see in your face that you don't think it would have been easy and I do know you are right. Things never are quite the way you expect when you are young. But, it doesn't matter. James left."

"He left?"

"He joined the Army and was shipped off to Canada. I doubt he would ever have returned if—if he had not become Doveshire."

CHAPTER FIVE

Linnette watched as Annabelle lifted the cartoon again, but rather than looking at it, Annabelle began to fold it, again and again, before beginning to speak. "I am not sure that I quite see the problem. You implied at the beginning that you were involved in some manner with Ja— with Doveshire, with the new duke."

How should she answer? How much could she say? "He is my lover. It is as plain as that, and I fear I grow too old to pretend." It sounded so simple when she said it. Words could not convey the way her heart had stopped when she'd first seen him again, weeks ago, the way she'd felt as if he'd never left, the way her body had burned for his touch from that first glance, the way—

God, her face must have been flaming as images of that night filled her. She doubted they'd spoken ten sentences between them before they'd found a dark corner in the back of the garden and her skirts had been about her waist. She could still see him standing before her half-naked. She could see the boy he'd been beneath the strong man's body he now inhabited. Even the nasty scar that marked his thigh and hip had not made him seem different. He was still her James.

"That is nonsense," Annabelle said, drawing Linnette's thoughts back to the present. "These things are never plain and easy, even I know that. And I must admit I am trifle shocked. I'd always heard the English were so reserved."

"Are you shocked that I have a lover or that I admit it?"

"I suppose that you admit it. I am not naive enough to think that these things only happen within the bonds of marriage." Annabelle looked down at her hands, her cheeks becoming flushed as if at her own thoughts.

"I am relieved to hear that." And Linnette was. She needed advice from a woman of some understanding. "I am still not sure what I am doing telling you these things. It is only that . . ." She hesitated, suddenly unsure.

"I take it as a great gift that you feel comfortable after such a short acquaintance. I must admit selfishly that it makes me feel much less alone. And even with my sister here, I have felt quite alone."

"Thank you. Would you take it amiss if I asked if we could partake in something a bit stronger than tea? My nerves have not quite settled this day. I know it is early, but—."

"Say no more." Annabelle quickly summoned the maid and asked for some sherry to be brought. "Unless you care for something even stronger . . ."

"No, sherry is quite fine, quite perfect, actually."

They waited in silence while the drink was brought and poured.

"I was feeling quite alone, also. I think that is what I was trying to find the words to say." Linnette took a deep sip of the dry sherry, letting it burn down her throat. "I have always had Kathryn to talk to, ever since we were small girls. It is a strange feeling when one no longer has one's closest friend to talk to."

"I had a friend like that back in Boston. Perhaps I should say 'have,' for we do correspond, and sometimes when I am writing her, I can almost hear her voice in my head, but it is not the same as when we were together."

"I can see that it is not." Linnette took another swallow. The sherry had warmed her chest now and she felt the first hint of relaxation. "I had never considered how hard it must be to leave all you know. I've lived in the same area for my entire life. My father's house in Mayfair is only a street away from Doveshire's and I've already described the estates. I've never left anyone behind. Although James did leave me."

"But he is back now."

"Yes, but he returned for the title, not for me. And it took him eight endless years." Only he had asked her to marry him, hadn't he? For the first time all day Linnette let the thought fill her mind.

James had asked her to marry him.

She couldn't do it, wouldn't do it, of course. But, still . . .

James had asked her to marry him—again.

"If you had such a great love, why did he leave? Or why didn't he come back earlier?" Annabelle leaned forward across the table, her eyes sparkling with curiosity.

Right to the heart of the issue. The marchioness certainly was not faint of heart. "I don't know. Perhaps he did not feel as I did. They say women often feel these things more strongly than men. To him I may have been nothing more than a spring-time memory. A fond one, I hope."

"And yet you welcomed him back to your bed within a few weeks of—."

"Within a few hours, perhaps minutes, to be honest. I saw him and it was not even a question. The moment we were alone— well, let us just say that there was not much conversation."

"I think that is your problem." Annabelle spoke with great surety.

"What?"

"Conversation, or rather lack of it. You need to ask the duke these questions."

"I tried."

"And?"

"He changed the subject." And how he'd changed the subject. But he had asked her to marry him.

It was impossible. Absolutely impossible.

What would people say? Not that she'd do it even if all of London cheered for her. The real issue was trust—she would never believe she could lean on him, rely on him.

"You don't seem the type of woman to let that stop you. Ask him again—and demand he answer." Annabelle stood, picked up the last drops of sherry in her glass, and held it high. "To men and getting answers."

Linnette followed Annabelle to her feet and held up her own glass. She chinked it against Annabelle's. "To answers."

Annabelle was right. She was having this conversation with the wrong person.

A kiss? He'd been seen kissing Linnette? James resisted the urge to turn and stare at Elizabeth. At Lady Smythe-Burke's?

It must have been that first kiss, when joy had driven away all thought. He remembered the occasion, certainly. He hadn't even known Linnette would be there, but then he'd seen her and her dress had been cut so low, her lips so full, her—well, he hadn't been able to help himself. Not that he ever had. Damn and blast. He was lucky that a kiss was all she'd seen. They'd tried so hard to be discreet ever since.

"Come and sit, Elizabeth. Your pacing is beginning to wear on me. And this is not a subject that needs to be discussed," Annie said. She turned to James with a smile and nodded to the settee. "And you should sit, too. We really must discuss funding for the orphanage. I refuse to let children suffer because of our petty disagreements."

Elizabeth seated herself, arranging her skirts with care. He took a seat on the settee beside her, careful to keep several feet between them. It was amazing how cowed he was beginning to feel as the two women began to explain in great detail the workings of the orphanage and all the ways he could, no, *must*, help. All he really wanted was for them to leave. He was tempted to offer them anything if only they'd go and leave him alone—to wait for Linnette, to think of Linnette.

The cushion of the settee dipped lower beside him, and he turned his head.

The longer they talked the nearer Elizabeth seemed to come. He never saw her move, but from having a couple of feet between them the space had diminished until it could be counted in inches. He was tempted to stand and pace, as well.

The heavy rose scent that the countess wore was tickling his nose. She turned to him with the slightest of smiles, explaining in a low, serious tone about the need for another pair of shoes for each child. Her eyes, however, were not serious. They spoke of something else, something he did not care to examine too closely.

He shifted slightly away, his hip pressing hard into the arm of the settee. Damn, he was not a man who desired pursuit and Elizabeth was making it all too clear that she saw him as some type of prey. He tried to inch further away, but there was no room.

Hell.

He turned to Annie, but she prattled on, unmindful of the game being played out before her.

"I am so pleased that you've decided to help us. I am quite sure that everyone will wish to donate when they know that you are continuing Doveshire's sponsorship," Elizabeth said as she leaned toward him, her shoulder brushing his arm.

"I am not sure that my help will make a difference. I am still more of a curiosity than anything," James answered. "I know hardly anyone."

"You know us." Looking at him from under her lashes, Elizabeth tried to convey some deep message. "Surely we count."

He'd been stalked by bears, attacked by wolves, and faced both down without the slightest flicker of fear. Now he felt a great desire to run.

The worst of it was that it made no sense. The blasted woman was beautiful, extraordinarily so. He should have enjoyed the game, if nothing else.

And under normal circumstances he would have, but not now. Not when—Linnette's heartless laughter still echoed in his mind. His hand clenched into a fist.

"You seem lost in thought. I do hope that I am not boring

you. Or perhaps it is all this talk of children. Men rarely seem entertained by such discussion. In truth, I think men are only interested in the making of them." She leaned forward, again bending low, placing a hand on his thigh.

He shot a look at Annie. She had turned in her chair and was gazing out the window. Without looking at them she rose. "Excuse me a moment, please. We must be leaving soon and I should like to refresh myself first. A good splash of water on my cheeks will do me wonders." She turned toward the door and left the room without another word. At least she left the door open.

Elizabeth did not seem to mind. She squeezed his thigh tighter and then moved her fingers higher. Smiling at him, she stared—and not at his face. "Yes, let me repeat Annie's words, we are so thankful for your help. If only there were some way that I could . . ."

That was too much. He grabbed her hand, intent on moving it far from his—

"James, we must . . ." Linnette rushed into the room—and stopped—her words trailing off. Her eyes took in the scene instantly and then focused slowly on his hand and Elizabeth's clasped together. Her eyes traced the length of his leg, judging just where those hands were likely to land. Her lips thinned.

Whatever she had been about to say was swallowed, held back deep in her throat. Her gaze rose to his and he read fierce anger, anger and steely determination—and hurt. He was lucky it was not her hand poised above his thighs or he might have found himself speaking a few tones higher. He felt his own anger at her fade as he absorbed the full range of her emotions.

"Doveshire." Linnette held each syllable, reminding him of

their early conversation—how much he liked hearing his name on her lips. Pleasing him had clearly lost all priority. "I didn't know you had guests."

"They, Elizabeth and Annie," he saw the color fade from Linnette's face at his words and attempted a correction, "Lady Westhampton and Lady Richard came to speak about the Orphanage of Lost Angels." Surely she could not be upset by that. "Lady Richard has just excused herself for a moment."

"I see."

"I do hope I—we have not caused a problem." Elizabeth's tone did not mirror her words. She made no move to increase the distance between them. If anything, she leaned closer, her heavy perfume smothering him.

He pulled his hand away from Elizabeth's, and stood. "Why don't I go and see what has become of Lady Richard?"

"I am sure she'll be back in just a moment," Linnette said. "And I don't imagine that she'd be happy to be bothered."

"Oh, yes. Of course." Damn. What was he thinking? You didn't bother women when they were refreshing themselves—unless it had been planned beforehand.

Elizabeth slowly rose to her feet, her movements almost languid. She smiled like a child eyeing a bonbon, her eyes caressing him before moving back to Linnette. "You seem a little flushed, my dear duchess. Is something bothering you?"

Before Linnette could answer, Annie entered the room. Her eyes darted from one to the other as she tried to understand the situation. "Are you ready to leave?" she asked Elizabeth, her gaze dropping to the floor.

"Aren't you even going to say hello, Annie?" Linnette took a step toward her, turning her back on Elizabeth—and him.

Annie looked up and met Linnette's gaze and something passed between them. "I am sorry, Linnette. I wasn't sure you'd want me to. I thought you might prefer to just ignore me, ignore all of this."

"Oh Annie, I do realize that none of this is your fault." It was impossible to miss that she did not include Elizabeth in the statement.

"I still can't help but feel part of it. I think even being at Annabelle's last week was enough. Nothing seems the same anymore." Annie's gaze fell back to her feet.

Linnette stepped forward and placed a hand on each of Annie's shoulders. James could almost see her mood gentle as she spoke. "I do understand—and I must talk to you about Annabelle. I just think that perhaps we can be of help to her. I think she may need friends very badly and you have always been an excellent friend."

"I do try."

Elizabeth coughed, drawing her back straight. "I am still here."

"Believe me. I am very aware of that." Linnette dropped her hands from Annie's shoulders, her anger returning, and turned, her voice cool. "I am curious why didn't you speak with me about the orphanage. I have been responsible for funding it for years—from long before my husband's death."

"I am afraid that was my doing." Annie stepped forward. "I was trying to make things easier for everyone."

Linnette raised a hand to her brow and James could feel the fatigue that lay behind her careful smile and studied voice. "Have you resolved everything or is there still room for my input? I do actually care about the orphanage."

James wished he could go back in time and force the ladies to speak with Linnette to begin with. "Doveshire will back whatever your wishes are," he said with some formality.

Had Elizabeth rolled her eyes behind Linnette's back? He rather thought she had. He would have called attention to it, only that would clearly do nothing but make the situation worse.

"Of course, we want to know what you think," Annie said with some firmness, and a glare at Elizabeth. "But right now we really must be going. I promised Lady Smythe-Burke we would pay a call and she does believe one must arrive an hour early to be on time. And she is a most generous patron of our Lost Angels."

"I suppose that Annie is correct. We must say our farewells. I do know how you hate for us to say goodbye." Elizabeth spoke with only the faintest undertone of sarcasm as she smiled at Linnette. Then she moved closer to James and looked up from those up-tilted dark eyes. "And I do hate to take my leave as well."

Hostility was just about bristling off Linnette by now. He wished he could soothe her, but instead took the time to say the proper farewells.

Linnette watched as James escorted Annie and Elizabeth to the door in the hall. What was the man thinking? Didn't he realize if you gave Elizabeth a smidge she'd take a mile—or more? No, he probably didn't. Men had always been attracted to Elizabeth, with her exotic looks, and never seemed to realize just how clever her mind could be. The only thing that put them off was her fierce demeanor.

Normally, Elizabeth seemed completely unaware of the admiration she generated. But things had changed these past weeks since she'd decided to take a lover. She was tired of waiting for her absent husband to return and had decided to try out a different kind of life—if only she'd chosen a target other than James.

It had been hard to hold back a cry when she'd entered James's office and found him alone with Elizabeth and Elizabeth's hand where it definitely should not have been.

And she had actually encouraged Elizabeth's desire to take a lover in the beginning. A woman could only wait for a man for so many years—assuming that the Earl of Westhampton ever planned on returning from his endless travels.

But now it had all come to this! What had Elizabeth been thinking with those blasted cartoons? Was it just to get her hands on James? This would not end well for anybody.

Damn it all.

Linnette's temples were pounding, and she wanted nothing as much as to crawl upstairs and under the covers—alone.

But first she needed to talk with James. Annabelle was right, confronting him was the only solution.

She didn't care if he was still angry. This had to be resolved. She had to know why he had left, why he had waited so long to return.

Only, damn it all.

She didn't want to talk—not now. She felt a complete shrew and was bound to act like one if pressed, and he always did seem to press. Perhaps she could let it wait—just a little longer.

"You wanted to speak?" James reentered the room.

She massaged her left temple, wishing the pain away, wishing she did not feel she was just delaying. "Yes, but not now."

"It was not what it looked like. I would never——."

"I do know that." And oddly enough, she did. There were so many ways she did not trust him, but his fidelity was not one of them. "I know clearly where the blame lies."

"I don't think that——."

She rubbed harder. "I believe you. I begin to realize that the one thing we have between us is truth. You still have not lied to me."

"That is true." He took a step toward her. "I must apologize—for this morning. It was not quite——."

God, she didn't want to discuss that now. They both needed to explain things that could not be explained. "No apologies are necessary." And then she saw from his expression that they were. "James, I do understand—and I actually quite enjoyed myself. Now why do we not slice out that piece of our lives and regard it as an aberration. We both acted out of character. I did not mean to hurt you."

"I know." His eyes remained serious. "Yet still I bleed."

There were no words she could say. Even if she could call back her laughter, she could not change her answer. She stared back at him, wishing once again that she could turn back time. "Perhaps I should apologize instead."

"Only if you truly did not mean it, if your answer is different."

Her gaze dropped. "I said 'yes' eight years ago. I will not again."

"So you will not lie, either." Now she heard the bitterness of his tone.

"Why have you never lied?" The question was out before she could tell herself to let the matter drop.

He answered slowly. "I don't think I've ever even considered the question. It has never occurred to me to lie. What would it serve?"

She turned her back to him and walked to the desk, staring down at the account books he had been reviewing—her account books. "I don't know. It just seems strange that we can have all of this distrust between us—and yet no lies."

"I do not distrust you."

"But you did."

"I don't know what you mean." His voice deepened.

"It is why you left me."

"Whatever makes you believe that?"

"I have had eight years to consider the matter and that is what it always comes down to. I can think of several things—or people—that might have made you leave, but it all comes down to a lack of trust in me. Whatever happened that forced you to go—and I do believe you felt forced—if you had trusted me to stay with you, no matter what, you would not have left."

CHAPTER SIX

She was right.

He had never considered it in that light before, but Linnette was right. He had not believed that she would stay with him—or at least that she would wish to. Things might have progressed too far for her to actually leave him, they might have married, might have had a child, but in the end he had always believed she would wish to leave, to have the life she had been born to.

Any remaining anger at her earlier laughter melted to nothing. Neither of them was without fault.

He watched as she bent over the desk, a finger skimming down the column of numbers. She chewed at her lower lip. Her heavy hair was swept up into a swirl of curls leaving her neck bare, the edging of thick lace at the top of her gown brushing against the few tendrils that had escaped.

She tapped a finger on the account book and then turned to him. "You do the addition in your head, with no need of paper to figure."

"Yes."

"I've never been able to do that—not in all these years of

keeping the accounts. I always have to scratch, and add, and add again to get the correct answer. I've never been able to just do it in my head."

"I remember." And he did. He could remember her sitting with her school books before her, pen in hand, trying so hard to find the answer that he could just see—and he'd always admired her for her effort, and for the fact that she always did find that answer, no matter how hard it might be.

"It makes my head ache to try—and it is aching already. It has not been an easy day."

"No, it has not. You came in wishing to talk. Do you wish to continue?" It was hard to ask when he did not know what he wished. There was more honesty between them at this moment than he could ever remember—but he was not sure he wanted her honest answers. They might reveal too much about himself.

She lifted a hand and rubbed her temple again. "We should. But, no, I do not wish to."

"Then what do you wish?"

"I wish you would tell me the truth—the whole truth." She moved around the desk toward him. "No, I do not even wish that right now. I wish a quiet dinner with only a few candles. I wish to sit by a fire, although the afternoon is warm. And I wish to go to my bed early and to sleep the whole night through without a single dream."

"I cannot grant the last, but I can leave and allow you the first two."

"No, you mistake my meaning." She took another step forward. "I wish you would stay and just be with me. No talk beyond the weather and catching up on each other's lives. Tell me more of your sister and your stepfather and I will tell you of my little niece. Have I told you that Judith has had a daughter? The plumpest, sweetest little thing you have ever seen. She makes me dream for things I should not. No, ignore that last. It is not the conversation for tonight either."

"You want me to stay?" He hated to sound dense, but it was hard to believe.

"Yes. I am tired of avoiding life, whatever we have between us cannot be hidden forever. Circumstance demands we have some relationship. Do you think we can just be together as we used to be, as friends? Do you remember those long summers when I would sit beside you while you fished in the stream? Those summer days when we could talk for hours about nothing?"

"I do." They were some of the happiest memories that he had. "And you were right."

"I was right."

"I did not trust that I could keep you happy. I did not trust you to keep wanting me. I know that is not the conversation that you wish for now, but it needs to be said. I was young and you were even younger. I knew that our dreams were not real, that the life we imagined could never be."

"Are you sure? I have never known what could be." She turned away from him. "But no. I do not wish to have this conversation tonight. Tonight I want to escape, to take one night and pretend that life is easy."

"If that is what you wish, that is how it shall be."

"I will tell cook that you are staying for dinner—and I will have a fire lit in the parlor. It may be silly, but it is what I want."

Something was brushing her nose. Her neck was aching, her head bent at the most impossible angle. Linnette opened her eyes slowly. The room was dark, only a few faint coals glowed on the hearth.

Where was she? Her own parlor, she saw, but why? The pillow beneath her head shifted and sighed.

James.

He was still here. Her face was pressed to his chest. Her sleep-muddled mind tried to remember the evening. A quiet and lovely dinner. Sitting by the fire, slightly too warm, but soft and relaxed. She'd read for a while and he'd glanced through some papers.

He'd told her, in more detail, of his sister, just married to the new vicar and expecting her first child. His stepfather lived with them and although growing old and a little blind still managed to find his way about the library. He must have memorized the books by now, but could never resist pulling them out and fingering through them.

She'd shown him the drawings of her niece that she'd done a few weeks ago in the park. They lacked the skill of a true artist, but she rather thought she'd captured something of the innocence and joy the child radiated.

And somehow they'd kept their hands off each other, managed to hold back the desire that still flickered with every glance.

Yes, it had been a most lovely evening, the sort of evening she'd once thought would fill her life and so rarely had— although her dreams had not ended with them asleep in the parlor.

A soft sigh escaped her lips at the thought.

"I should be going." The words rumbled from deep within James's throat.

She turned her face to stare up at him. His normally smooth-shaven jaw was beginning to bristle and she had to curl her fingers to keep from stroking.

Not touching him had been the hardest part of the evening. Whenever he'd drawn close or their eyes had held for that second too long she'd wanted to stroke, to touch, to revel in having him close—but she'd resisted. She knew too well what a single touch could lead to.

Memories of their encounter that morning filled her and she was glad he could not see her blush. She still did not know how to feel about the whole affair. "What time is it?" she asked.

"I am not sure. Given that the coals of the fire are still glowing it cannot be as late as it seems, but if I do not leave now, I will not." His voice trailed off at the end as if awaiting her response.

There was temptation to tell him to stay, but she dared not.

She did not know what she wanted and there were too many questions left unanswered between them.

And there was the cartoon. She doubted that anyone was watching the house, but they could not be too careful before they decided what path to take.

She might very well decide to throw all caution into the wind, but if she did, that it would be with intent, not by mistake or through carelessness. "Yes, perhaps you had best go. It is late and the servants will have enough to gossip about."

"It was not by chance that they left the door open half a foot after clearing the port and glasses."

"No, I am sure it was not. They do tend to be protective even when there is no need."

"It is probably best that they did. Even I draw the line at debauchery with the servants watching."

She smiled. "You sound very like my mother when you say that, and I would never have believed that any such similarity was possible."

"It gives me shivers, but I am afraid you might be right. Not, of course, that I mean any disrespect to your mother. She was a lovely woman. I was sorry to hear of her passing."

"Thank you." She pushed herself upright, away from him, longing for his warmth the moment it was gone. "I do miss her."

"Well, I'd best be leaving." He made no move to stand.

She forced herself to her feet, going to stand at the window, looking out into the darkness, pretending she did not miss the heat of his touch.

There was no sound of movement behind her.

"What do you want from me?" She asked the question quietly.

"I told you what I wanted this morning and you laughed." Now she did hear him move, heard him stand and stretch.

"You were serious." Still, she did not turn to look at him.

"Yes, I do believe I was."

She had no answer for that. Marriage? To James? Now? It was a preposterous thought, but one that drew her. "I am sorry I laughed."

"It is I who should be sorry. I had no right to treat you like that no matter the provocation."

"Did I seem upset?"

"I am not sure. I did not stay long enough to inquire."

"Now for that you may be sorry. As I am sorry that I laughed. It was all so unexpected."

She heard his footsteps as he approached. "I truly will leave now, Linnette. I sense that we could talk in circles this evening."

"You may be correct. We do need to finish this discussion, but sometime when we are both bright and awake. I want no more misunderstandings."

His hand came rest upon her shoulder. His thumb moved with its own magic.

She turned her face, and looked up at him over her shoulder.

He held her eyes for a moment and then turned and left, leaving only quiet behind.

He should leave. James knew it was the only choice. It was what she wanted, but his feet slowed as his boots clicked against the marble tile of the entry floor.

They did need to talk.

He needed to talk.

Would there ever be a better time than now, now when their emotions were soft, their passions checked? If he waited, this moment might never come again. Their next meeting would be filled again with passion and want and—and confusion.

Now, at this moment, he was not confused.

For the first time in eight years he might begin to understand.

He pivoted and walked back to the parlor. Linnette stood still staring out the window as if hoping to see him walking down the path.

"Your father and the duke, Charles's father, forced me to go," he said the words flatly, not allowing emotion to seep into them. "They threatened my stepfather's living, said they would give the parish to someone else. I did not truly believe them, but I could not take the risk. And your father said he would never consent to any marriage between us. You were young. He could have dissolved any union we tried to form."

Her eyebrows lifted for a moment, surprise shining on her face, and then her features settled, her thoughts moving forward. "We could have eloped, fled to Scotland."

"And what then? If we returned, he would have done his best to separate us. You were so young."

"As were you." Still she stared out the window and it was impossible to read her tone.

"Yes, but I was old enough to fear—to fear that we could not last, that love was not enough."

She sighed, long and deep. "I can understand that now. I could not have then. But it doesn't matter. What is done is done." She did not turn.

"It does matter. I meant it when I asked you to marry me this morning. We can put the past behind us, begin again."

"And what of gossip and innuendo? The Dowager and the Duke. It does have quite the ring."

"I certainly do not care. Do you?"

"You have explained why you left, but not why you did not return. Why did you stay away for eight years?"

He had waited all day for her to ask again and still he had no answer. "I don't know."

She turned then and walked toward him slowly, hips swaying, russet curls glinting by the light of the single candle. It was hard to see her face, to see her thoughts, but it was clear she knew the temptation she offered. "I think you do. Was I not enough for you? What did Canada offer that I could not?"

"It was not like that."

"Then what was it like? What did you want that I could not supply?" Her voice was low and husky, wrapping about him, drawing him closer. "Do you know that for eight years I dreamed of you, dreamed of those few stolen hours we had together? Do you know how guilty I felt throughout my marriage that I could never forget you, forget how you made me feel?"

"I did not know."

"And would it have changed things if you did? I don't think I believe that it would have. You came back for the title, not for me." It was impossible to mistake the bitterness that filled her.

He took a step forward, held out his hand. "It is true that I came because of the dukedom. I had no choice. I have never been able to turn my back on responsibility."

"As you turned your back on me? You slept with me, took my virginity, made me love you—and then you left with no word." Were those tears glinting on her cheeks?

"Your father and the duke demanded—."

"And their demands were more important than my feelings, my concerns?"

"I wrote you—I tried to explain."

"I never received a letter—not a single one in all those years."

"I know." He looked away for a second, and then turned his gaze back. "After the first one, hell, the first six I wrote, I received a brief note from your father saying that you had married Charles and that he and the duke would be sure that you never received a single note I posted."

Yes, those were tears. Her cheeks shone silver in the candlelight as she lifted her face to him. "And after Charles's death, when I was managing the dukedom. Did you never think to write then?"

"I was afraid." He said the words he had refused to even think. "I knew that I had hurt you. I had tried to deny it, even to myself, for years but I knew what I had done. I doubted that you would forgive me."

"I would have forgiven you anything those first years."

"And now?"

She was still. He could see the thoughts playing across her face.

"And now?" he asked again.

"And now—I do not know. I do forgive you. I do understand."

"But . . ." He let the word hang.

"But I do not trust you." She smiled, but not with happiness. "I trust completely that you will not lie to me, but I do not believe that I can rely on you, lean on you."

"This is why you do not wish to marry me?" He began to understand.

"I believe I do wish to marry you—do not look like that, I have not finished. I do wish to marry you, but I do not believe it would be wise and I am at an age where wisdom is important."

"You sound like an old woman."

"Sometimes I feel like one. I have been on my own for many years. Even when I was married to Charles, I knew that I must watch out for myself. And while I did not know what my father had done, I had long realized that what he believed was best for me and what I believed was often quite different. I like being responsible to no one and having no one responsible for me."

"Don't you want children? I saw your face when you talked about your niece."

Her eyes grew dark and hard to read. "I am not willing to plan my life around something that might never be. Even if I married, who is to say there would be children? I was married for almost four years and it never happened. I have no reason to think it would be different now."

"But it might be."

"I will not live my life on a might."

"So the cartoons really don't matter? They are only an excuse?"

She stepped toward him and laid a hand upon his cheek, her fingers rubbing across the heavy stubble. "They matter. They force me to a decision. I must decide if we are worth the bother they will cause. I have been about in society for too long to believe that we can keep our relationship a secret once everybody is watching and curious—although it is hard because avoiding you would also cause gossip."

"So?" He felt anger rising and did not quite know why. What she said made sense, only . . .

"So I don't know. It's been only a single day. Why does the world demand an answer now?"

"It is not the world asking. I am the one asking."

"Then why does it feel like the world? Don't you understand? I don't want you to be my world—I let you become my world once and then you were gone. I want to stay free, as I have been these last four years."

"And if that is not possible? Even if we never spoke again, your life is changed. I am back, and I say that as Doveshire and not James. You will no longer manage the dukedom by yourself. You are not as powerful as you were a month ago—or as free. Do you really wish to run to the country and hide in a dower house? Is that the freedom you wish?"

She stepped back, her posture stiff. "Do you threaten me? If I will not marry you, you will turn against me?"

God, she could be infuriating. That was not what he had meant at all. "No. I was only stating fact. I am back. Even if I did nothing but drink and gamble all day, people would come to me for decisions. I am Doveshire." He said it with more force than ever before, for the first time the understanding of what it meant sinking into his bones.

"Do you think I do not know that? I told you this morning that I could feel the difference in how I was treated. I know damn well that, despite having had the title for years, I am only now truly the dowager."

"And is that freedom? Marry me and you will just be the duchess again, have the power again. It is not too late for us."

She stared into his face as if searching for more words. There was something she wanted, something he was not giving. "I cannot marry you. I do not want to marry again a man I cannot rely on to put me first."

"And what can I do to show you that I put you first?"

"Slay a dragon?" She said it as a joke, but he felt the truth of her words. She was looking for some great task that would allow him to prove himself, allow her to trust him again.

"I haven't seen many dragons about."

She did not answer.

"And if I do not find a dragon? What then? Do you wish me to marry another?"

Still, she did not answer.

"I may not have started with much loyalty to the title, but I am damned if I'll have them go heir hunting again just because you will not be reasonable. The title is mine for life, but after that? I must be responsible. I can't imagine leaving it to a rat like Swatts or any offspring he may have."

That caught her. "I am not unreasonable. If anything, I think I am too reasonable."

"Then damn it all. I'll be reasonable too. I'll find myself a wife and have a dozen children. And you can stand at the gates of the dower house and watch them play upon my lawns."

This time when he left he did not turn back.

THE MAIDS

Jane stood outside the kitchen windows and waved frantically for Abby. She had to tell her what had just happened. She still could not believe it. Lady Westhampton and Lady Richard had taken tea with Lady Smythe-Burke and she, Miss Jane White, had served them.

She'd felt wonderful in the past sharing some tidbit that her sister had passed on, but this time she'd spoken to them herself. It might only have been asking if the biscuits were fine and if they needed anything else, but she'd spoken to them.

The kitchen door creaked open and before Abby could even stick her head out, Jane found herself spilling out the story. " . . . And Lady Smythe-Burke had me stay in the room. They'd just been to the Duke of Doveshire's house. Can you imagine them all together? Well, of course, not Lady Harrington—we know they're not speaking—and the dowager duchess only came in at the end. Lady Richard was quite kind about her, but Lady Westhampton made some catty comment about how she was looking at the duke."

"Who was looking at the duke?" Abby was clearly not paying enough attention.

"The dowager duchess, of course. They didn't say if she looked like she was with child, but I almost begin to think she might be—and the duke is so handsome. Lady Westhampton flushed whenever she said his name. I wonder if she might have an affection for him herself."

"That would be something," Abby replied.

Jane considered for a moment. "Lady Westhampton is married, for all that means. Do you think she'd really be after the duke?"

"As you said, he is handsome. Do you think he might call on Lady Smyth-Burke? I think I'd swoon if I saw him."

"Gentlemen don't call on her nearly as often as ladies."

Abby sighed.

Jane knew just how she felt. She glanced up at the sun. "I'd best be getting back. I am supposed to be taking a note to Lady Carrington, but I could not resist the chance to tell you."

"Then you'd best be off. We can meet again in the morning."

"Yes. I wonder what will be up in the windows tomorrow. It's hard to imagine anything more scandalous than yesterday morning's."

Abby slipped back into the kitchen with a smile. "I wonder . . ."

CHAPTER SEVEN

It was a beautiful day for a walk. The sun shone brightly, even for an early summer day, and the sky was a deep, clear blue. A gentle breeze blew to keep the air from growing too warm and the trees were fully leafed, casting great circles of shade.

Linnette did not care. She kept hearing James's words of the night before replaying in her head.

Was she being a fool?

She strode forward, arms swinging. She looked back over her shoulder, glancing at her maid hurrying behind. She was not in the mood for a stroll, she wanted a walk, something brisk and fast that stirred the blood and cleared the mind.

She smiled, big and wide and strictly for herself, trying to convince herself that all was well.

The worries of the world were still heavy on her shoulders, but she would avoid them—at least for the rest of the morning.

She chose a path heading down to the water, hoping the beauty of the lake would quiet her thoughts.

There were ducks on the lake, mothers swimming serenely with a trail of half-grown ducklings trailing behind. A nurse with two small children sat on a bench, the youngest girl diligently breaking bread into small pieces. She was about the same age as Linnette's niece and Linnette found her feet slowing.

What would it be like to have a child, a little daughter of her own? She could so easily imagine walking down here most mornings with her daughter's hand tucked tight inside her own, imagine the laughter and the fun.

It had been years since she'd indulged in such thoughts. When Charles had lived, she'd often imagined the children that were to come, the sturdy little boy, heir to the dukedom, and the daughter with a smile that could fill her face, perhaps with Charles's dark curls.

Since Charles's death, she hadn't even dreamed of owning a dog.

The estates had been all she needed, all she cared about.

Even when she'd taken a lover it had been without dreams of the future. She'd understood the exact limits of each relationship. It was probably why such liaisons had all lost their attraction and she'd decided to be happy on her own.

Then James had returned—James and his questions.

The little girl had gathered her crumbs in her skirts and stood on the stone edging to the water. The ducks turned mid-paddle and hurried in her direction, clearly understanding what was to come. They quacked loudly, squabbling for position as the girl began to throw handfuls of crumbs into the water.

James had truly asked if she wanted to marry him? He'd asked if she wanted children?

Why did her heart and her brain give her different answers?

Linnette turned from the happy child and began to stride

along the path about the lake. What did she want? She'd given up waiting for James to return when she'd married and then for a second time about a year after her husband's death. She'd always known deep in her heart that he would never come back when she was wed to another.

But why hadn't he come back before now? Did she believe that he had merely been afraid? It seemed unbelievable—and yet it rang true. Could a man who seemed afraid of nothing truly fear her?

And why did she still fear that he'd come back for the title and not for her?

She batted her eyelashes at the thought, turning her face into the breeze, denying the feeling of betrayal that came with it. He was not worth her tears. She'd given him enough of them eight years ago.

So what did she want?

How could she want a dream she didn't believe in?

How could she marry a man she did not fully trust?

James had admitted that part of why he'd left was that he hadn't believed she would stay with him and be happy. Well, he'd proved to her already that he wasn't willing to stay just for her. How could she ever trust that now would be different?

And what if he truly had been afraid? Was that enough of a reason?

Her mind churned in endless circles of questions.

"Is that her?"

Linnette slowed as the loud question intruded on her thoughts, turning to see who had spoken.

Several young women stood grouped in a tight circle, their eyes all on her. One blushed as Linnette's gaze caught her. One of her companions leaned over and whispered something in her ear. The young woman's gaze dropped with unmistakable interest to Linnette's belly and then back to her face. And then they giggled. It was impossible to tell who began it but the tittering seemed to emanate from them in a solid wave.

Linnette suddenly felt great sympathy for James's anger at her laughter yesterday morning.

She almost grabbed her dress and pulled it tight, eager to show off her slender frame. Annabelle had been right, current fashion made it seem possible she really did have a belly the size of large melon under her dress.

She did not need this. She'd been overly emotional before, lack of sleep and lack of decision eating away at her normally orderly mind.

She turned away and strode on further, faster, not bothering to look back for her maid. Given all the gossip and those blasted cartoons, what did it matter if she ended up walking alone? That was not going to ruin her reputation—at least not any further than it already was.

She had never been laughed at before and was amazed at how deeply it stung.

This walk was not providing the peace she had sought. First the little girl and the memories she'd sparked, and now the realization that she truly was being gossiped about and laughed at.

It had been easy to believe she could be strong in the face of ridicule—before she'd felt it.

She turned a corner, coming around a large boxwood—and stopped. Before her on the path stood Annie, Elizabeth—and Kathryn—Kathryn and a very large and playful puppy. What were they doing here? It should be hours before fashionable ladies began to stroll.

She stood, staring. Kathryn stopped also—then took a single step toward her, pulling hard at the dog's lead.

Neither of them spoke.

Elizabeth came up behind Kathryn, catching her arm and attempting to turn her away, but Kathryn would not be moved. Instead she handed the dog's lead to Elizabeth and moved toward Linnette.

Linnette pulled a deep breath into her chest, held it, then stepped toward her friend. Perhaps this small thing she might be able to fix.

"I am so sorry. I should have told you about what happened with Harrington. No, I should never have been involved with your husband in the first place—even if he wasn't your husband then. No, I should never have been involved with him and I should have told you."

The corners of Kathryn's mouth tilted up, although her eyes remained serious. "That makes no sense."

"I know, I am just so sorry."

"Come away. There's no need to upset yourself." Elizabeth was pulling at Kathryn's arm again—and at the same time pulling at the puppy, who clearly had other ideas.

"I am not upset." Kathryn took a step toward Linnette. "I've been looking for a way to speak with you. I just didn't expect it would be here, in the park. I don't ever come this early in the day— except now with Fifi," she nodded at the puppy, "I have to come before the crowds or there is bound to be trouble. She ruined more skirts with her muddy paws than I can bear to think about."

Linnette glanced at the dog, which had rolled on its back

and was wiggling with abandon. Elizabeth was doing her best to pretend nothing was happening.

Kathryn caught her glance. "She's a wolfhound, a gift from Harrington—but that is a story for later, when all this is behind us."

"I thought you never wanted to speak to me again," Linnette said.

"And how many times have we said that to each other over the years?" Kathryn answered.

"I do remember when you stole my red rubber ball the very day my father gave it to me."

"I believe I was only three at the time. And you had taken my favorite stuffed bear."

"You were too old for bears." Linnette felt her heart lighten with each word of banter.

"I was three."

"I remember you as older."

"Well, what about the time you told me that sitting in the sun would clear up my pimples and all it did was give me freckles?" Kathryn was not ready to concede the point.

"So we are speaking again?"

"I must say that sleeping with my husband is a good step worse than causing my nose to freckle, but I will admit that given that it was over a year before I met the man, I can only stay angry for so long."

"I should have told you," Linnette said the words quietly, but with great emphasis.

"Yes, you should have. I can see that it was difficult, but you should not have left me to find out the way I did—from that foul cartoon."

Linnette took a slight step back so that her gaze captured Annie and Elizabeth as well. "Has there been any further news of the cartoons? Of who is behind them?" She narrowed her eyes at Elizabeth as she spoke.

"No," Annie spoke up. "I've asked around to the extent possible and nobody seems to know."

"I have made inquiries also and everybody seems baffled—and eager for the next one," Kathryn said.

All four women were quiet for a moment as they considered that thought.

"I spoke with Annabelle yesterday," Linnette said. "She, too, knows nothing more."

"I thought after the last cartoon that they were aimed at me and Harrington," Kathryn leaned closer, "but after this last one I fear they may be aimed at you, Linnette."

"But why? What have I ever done to cause such anger?"

"I can think of some things." Elizabeth stepped forward, dragging the dog. "Are you really going to forgive her with such ease, Kathryn? I am not sure I would ever forgive her."

What was Elizabeth's problem? Whatever it was it did not need to be aired here, in front of the others. "Why don't you come look at the ducks with me, Elizabeth?" Linnette asked, trying to draw her away, to talk to her with more privacy.

"I'll come too." Annie clearly sensed trouble in the air and, as always, was trying to diffuse it.

"No, why don't you stay and keep Kathryn company," Elizabeth said. She thrust the dog's lead at Annie and grabbed hold of Linnette's arm. "We will be fine by ourselves."

Linnette smiled sweetly at her friends and walked off toward the water, dragging Elizabeth along.

The moment they were out of earshot she turned and faced Elizabeth. "Why did you do it? I can understand wanting to hurt me, but the first cartoon hurt Kathryn far more than it upset me."

"I don't know about that," Elizabeth responded. "I saw your face at Annabelle's when I first brought out the cartoon of you and Harrington. You were not at all pleased."

"I was upset for Kathryn. I knew how it would hurt her. There had been rumors about Harrington and me for years. It was old news, nobody would have cared—nobody but Kathryn."

"I don't know about that either. Look about you now. Everyone is speculating. I do believe Mrs. Wattington is staring at your belly as we speak and trying to decide if it has grown. The prospect of an unwed dowager duchess having a child is quite entertaining."

Linnette glanced in the direction where Elizabeth had nodded. Mrs. Wattington stood there making no pretense that she was not staring at the two of them. Linnette glanced down at her bell-shaped skirt and swore. Current fashion would be the death of her.

She glanced about. Elizabeth and she were the center of attention and not one eye seemed focused on Elizabeth. "Is this what you wanted?" she asked. "I still don't understand why you are so upset with me."

Elizabeth drew in a long, deep breath. Her gaze followed the path that Linnette's had. A slight smile formed on her lips. "I cannot say that I am sorry for your troubles. Everything has always been so easy for you. You had a handsome husband, a grand title, and all you've ever had to do is look at a man and he was yours. I've had to work for everything I've ever received and no man has ever looked at me the way they do at you. If anything, they avoid me."

"Is that why your husband left and never returned?" Linnette regretted the words as soon as they were spoken, but there was no calling them back. Elizabeth was extremely attractive to men, whether or not she realized it.

"Why my husband left is no concern of yours." Elizabeth had grown a good three shades paler, but her eyes still sparked with anger.

"Maybe if you didn't look ready to attack all the time, men would not be afraid to approach you."

"How can they when they are so busy watching you wiggle your hips across a room? And your breasts. Have you ever considered buying a dress that has enough fabric to cover them?" Elizabeth stepped back and up onto the low rock wall that edged the lake, raising her several inches higher than Linnette.

"My dresses have nothing to do with whether men look at you or don't. Although perhaps if you had some breasts to show, they'd pay more attention." Why was she acting so catty? Linnette had always taken pride in never resorting to such tactics, but Elizabeth was bringing out the worst in her. She stepped up on the wall beside Elizabeth, refusing to cede any unnecessary height advantage to her foe.

Elizabeth set her lips in a tight line and glared.

Linnette glared back. She was sure they were putting on quite a show for the gossiping biddies.

"So is it your breasts that attracted Doveshire or just your easy ways?" Elizabeth just about spit the words at her.

"I am not sure which Doveshire you mean, but I can promise you they both liked my breasts—and both would have told you I was anything but easy." She was so tempted to push Elizabeth into the water. "But, I think what they like best is that I am not a bitch. I'd never betray my friends like you have."

"I have never betrayed my friends. That is you. First, Kathryn and now me."

"How did I ever betray you? —and I don't admit to betraying Kathryn. That was all years ago."

"How did you betray me? I tell you that I am ready to take a lover and that I think the new Doveshire is the man for me and within the hour you're leading him into a dark garden. Can't you bear to let anyone else have a man or do you need to claim them all?"

"It wasn't like that—and even if it had been, that is quite different than planting these evil lies."

"You've already admitted that it wasn't a lie about Harrington and from what I've seen it isn't a lie about Doveshire. You practically drool when you look at him."

She *was* going to push Elizabeth. She couldn't wait to see her splashing in the water, her sodden dress clinging to her. And then a far better plan formed. She glanced around. Nobody was watching closely, attentions had wandered, but neither was anybody leaving if the possibility of a story existed. Oh, she'd give them a story.

"Just tell me why you did it? Why the cartoons? Why hurt Kathryn as well?" Linnette took a small step closer to Elizabeth, positioned herself just right.

"I did not do it. Oh, I can't say I am sorry at the outcome.

Kathryn seems to have recovered well and I do love how everybody stares at you and titters. It's about time people saw what you're really like."

"I don't believe you. Nobody else would be so spiteful." Linnette glanced back, prepared herself. She didn't know why Elizabeth was denying it. There really was no other possibility.

"I tell you I didn't do it. If I had I would have—." Elizabeth took a half-step forward.

This was the moment.

Linnette threw up her hands, and screamed as loudly as she could. "No, no, don't do it!" She stepped backwards off the wall, letting herself fall into the water below.

It was far shallower than she had realized—and colder. She was lucky she hadn't cracked her head on one of the scattered rocks. It would probably have served her right, but she couldn't regret her actions.

She rose from the hip-deep water and glared up at Elizabeth who stood looking down at her shock.

"How *could* you?" Linnette asked loudly, doing her best to draw everybody's attention—although she imagined her scream and splash had already accomplished that.

"But, I—I didn't!" Elizabeth was too shocked to form a coherent thought. Her face was blank as she stared down at Linnette.

Linnette trudged back to the wall and with some small difficulty climbed back up onto the wall. "Oh, but I assure you, you did." She let Elizabeth see the slightest hint of a smile before she let her face fall. She looked down at her dress and yelled, "My dress. My new dress. You've ruined it." With each word she brushed the fabric down, pulling it tight. The soft muslin clung to her, nearly transparent. "Look at me. I am such a horror."

She twisted this way and that looking down at her skirts, but also glancing at the gathering crowd. Nobody would think she had a belly now. The full skirts were so tight about her body it would be impossible to think she had anything to hide.

She turned from Elizabeth and walked with great dignity toward Annie and Kathryn—and the dog, which wagged its tail, clearly enjoying the show. Each step was slow and careful, allowing everyone to have a good gander, to see just how slender she was.

CHAPTER EIGHT

"You're here?" Linnette's voice echoed as she entered, pushing aside the heavy curtains that draped all sides of the opera box. Her tone was much more civil than he would have expected given how they had parted.

"Where else would I be?" James stood as she approached, his gaze taking in the deep blue gown and flash of diamonds. Her hair was upswept this evening, curls escaping at her brow and the sparkle of more diamonds caught in the waves. She truly was a duchess this evening—if not a queen.

"Off risking it all on the turn of card, or looking for that young chit to marry. I didn't know you cared for music."

"I don't. And you know I didn't mean it about the marriage." He said it slowly, letting his gaze show her just what he did care for. It might be a mistake. He'd spent the afternoon trying to decide how to handle this aggravating woman who would not be his wife. And he'd finally come to the realization that he'd take her however he could get her—and he'd keep looking for that dragon to slay.

"How did you know I'd be here? I would have thought you would avoid me. When you left, I wasn't sure you'd ever wish to see me again." She took a seat beside his at the front of the box. He could tell she was on edge.

"I remembered how you always longed to attend the opera when you were a girl. It didn't seem like the sort of thing that would have changed. And I've given up on avoiding you—and arguing with you—and accepted that I cannot resist you."

She pressed her lips together, but he could see the glint in her eye. His answer had pleased her.

And just like that he knew they had survived their argument of the morning. Things might not be easy between them, but they were progressing.

"Did you invite any other guests?" he asked.

"No. I had planned to—but—."

"But?"

"It was a strange afternoon."

"A good one?"

"I am not sure yet. It has left me most unsettled."

"Do you wish to discuss it?"

"I am not sure that I do." She peered over the high edge of the balcony, looking intently at the crowd that was very intently staring at her. "Although there may be no avoiding it."

"Is it still the cartoon? I would admit to getting my share of strange looks and ribbing throughout the day."

"It is that—but it's more than that. I am afraid I courted my own share of gossip this afternoon. I am surprised you have not heard."

"I spent most of the afternoon at home reviewing the plans for the fall harvest. I stopped by my club but only briefly. I assumed any strange looks related to the cartoon. What have you done?"

Linnette leaned forward, bending over the railing. "I am tempted to wave. I've never been such the center of attention. Even when I first appeared after marrying Charles people only stared for a moment. Now I feel they are waiting for me to do something scandalous. I am surprised Lady Beard has not trained her opera glasses upon us. She certainly has not taken her eyes off me. Should I pull tight my skirts and show her my flat belly?"

"You are in a strange mood."

She reclined in her chair, letting her head fall back. "I think I am just tired, tired of fighting with you, tired of never knowing where I stand—and tired of all this." She gestured towards the audience.

"I am tired of fighting also. I surrender. We can play this game as you wish—and I will never marry another as long as you are with me. I will let my cousin Swatts inherit the title after me, if I must."

"Given that he is a good ten years older than you, that may not be a worry."

"Well then, whoever comes after him. You may end up running the dukedom again while they look for him."

"Don't even say that." She placed a hand on his sleeve and he could think of nothing but her.

"So what do you want?" he asked.

"I am not sure I know what you mean." Her fingers stroked the thick fabric of his sleeve and he could almost pretend they were stroking something else.

"Do we hide? Should I leave and go talk to some other sweet young thing to protect your reputation? Perhaps I can invite someone else to join us. I see that Tattingstong has just arrived with his wife. You did mention you had become friends."

Linnette leaned forward a bit. He watched as she considered the matter.

"I think perhaps we should just let them be. I do want to help Annabelle. I have promised to do so, but I think perhaps this is not the best moment. I do not want to cause her any more difficulties when I am so mired in gossip. I will send her a note."

It took but a moment to summon a servant and take care of the matter.

Linnette watched as across the way her note was received and read. James watched as eyes met and the ladies exchanged a slight nod.

Shifting in her chair, Linnette leaned back again. "Ahh, I am glad that worked. I confess I did not want to feel guilty for not helping her, but I also did not wish company—not when we have so much unresolved between us." She leaned toward him, her hand once again finding his sleeve. Her fingers brushed the fabric back and forth slowly, working their way down to edge of lace at his wrist.

He shivered as she brushed his bare skin.

Turning in his chair so that he could stare at her more directly, he felt the corners of his mouth lift. "Is this a sign that you are forgiving me, my lady?"

Her eyes clouded. "In truth, I don't know. It is certainly a sign that I am not happy when I am not touching you, near to you, but forgiveness—I do not know. And forgiveness for what?"

"That is the question. Forgiveness for my storming away earlier?"

"I talked with Kathryn today in the park. It was only for a few moments, but she reminded me of all the ways we have slighted each other over the years and how none of it matters. We are as much family as friends. So yes, I forgive you for being a boar. I daresay I was one too. But in truth you are as much my family as you are my lover. Day-to-day arguments and fights do not truly matter between us."

"But you will not let me truly be your family." He said the words with more anger than he meant.

"Do not feel that way. That is not a matter of forgiveness."

He started to turn away, but she lifted her other hand to his cheek and held his face, staring deep into his eyes.

"You will cause talk," he said, but he did not pull from her hands.

"I am reaching the point where I do not care." She rubbed her fingers across his cheek. "You shaved just before coming."

"Yes, and I do not believe you do not care."

She turned her head and stared out at the crowd just as the lights were extinguished and the performance began. "Well, I wish not to care."

He turned his head and laid a kiss upon her palm. "I know."

"But, you are right—sometimes I care too much. I am working on not caring, however." Her eyes met his again and he could swear he saw a sparkle.

The music began and for a moment they were silent.

Linnette reached out and began playing with the tie of the curtain at the front of the box, her fingers twisting the heavy silk cord, unmindful when the cord pulled loose and the curtain fell part way forward.

Then, for no reason he could understand, she stood, pulling away from him, and for a moment he feared he had lost her, that she had decided to avoid all gossip, that it all had been too much for her.

Shaking her skirts, she turned and walked towards the two sets of curtains that closed the balcony from the hall. She tripped on the step, her clumsiness so different than her usual grace, and the loud clatter of her heels drew all eyes to her, despite the gentle rise of the music. They continued to follow her as she moved toward the double set of curtains that blocked the hall. She stood for a moment, her pale skin highlighted in the castoff glow of the stage.

He wanted to call her back, but having no idea what had prompted her to leave he did not know what to say.

She stepped into the darkness of the drapes, and he knew he had lost his chance.

The velvet curtains swayed and billowed.

All eyes turned back to the stage and away from the disappearing duchess.

He forced his own glance away, staring out at the crowd, pretending he saw anything but her straight back as she left.

Something caught deep in his chest.

Had he lost her?

A floorboard creaked, almost inaudible beneath the swell of the music.

He turned his head back—and he saw her—saw Linnette standing half behind the heavy drapes that blocked the exit, deep in the shadows.

"Wha—?" He started to speak, but she held up a single finger, silencing him.

Was she really going to do this?

She was.

Something had gotten into her this day and she wasn't quite sure what, wasn't sure what was pushing her to act in such unthinkable ways.

First, Elizabeth and the lake—and now this.

No, she wasn't sure what—but she was beginning to think that she liked it.

There were some definite mixed feelings about what had happened with Elizabeth. But this was not the time for those.

She was going to do this because it was the right thing, because it was needed. James had said they would play the game as she wished and this was most definitely what she wished.

She flattened herself against the wall, hidden from wide view by the curtain she had loosened. She slid against the wall, praying that only James could see her return.

James was still staring at her, and she gestured for him to turn back to the stage. He raised a brow, but did so—his eyes still doing their best to follow her, even as he faced the stage.

She could feel James's peering at her from the corner of his eyes and it gave her courage. He was trying to keep his head turned forward, but she could tell he wanted to turn and ask what she was doing. She lifted her head and smiled, slowly but with clear purpose, keeping her intentions in mind, letting her every move show just what she wanted, what she needed.

She slid forward another step, her movements slow and sensuous. And then she was beside him. Keeping her back straight against the wall, she lowered herself with care until her knees touched the floor. She looked down a moment, and then raised her eyes to his, staring up at him from her spot kneeling on the floor. Pulling in a deep breath, she moved slightly until she was before him, the high front of the balcony blocking her from all view but his.

Unable to wait any longer, she ran a hand up each of his calves, her fingers massaging the muscles as she went. His whole body stilled, as James finally understood her design.

"I don't believe this is wise," he whispered.

Not wise? No, this was not wise. And she didn't care. Ever since James had left her eight years before she'd done things because they were wise.

She'd married Charles because it was the thing to do.

She'd carried on when he died because it was necessary.

She'd been ready to welcome the new duke and retire gracefully to the country because she didn't want to be a bother.

She'd continued managing the estates when he chose to stay in India because what else could she do?

She'd kept on when he died because there had been little choice.

And then James had arrived. And all her choices seemed meaningless.

Oh, she could not deny she hadn't come to enjoy running the estates, relished the power, but she had not done any of it because it was what she wanted.

If she'd done what she wanted, she would have sailed after James and let him know just what she thought of his desertion. The army would have shot him if he'd deserted it the way he deserted her. She might have shot him, also. She just would have aimed differently.

"What are you thinking? You have the strangest expression

on your face," James asked, speaking so quietly it was hard to hear.

"I am thinking that you are very lucky that I did not meet up with you soon after you left or what is about to happen would have been impossible."

She slid her hands from his knees, where they had come to rest, up his thighs. She watched him swallow and then diverted her eyes lower. "Yes, it would have been most unfortunate if I'd fulfilled my dreams in those months after you deserted me."

"You are never going to forgive me, are you?"

"I have already forgiven you. That should be evident." She let her hands slip even higher, stroking the lush fabric of his trousers, feeling his shivers as she let her thumbs explore his sensitive inner thighs.

"It would seem so, but I am not sure."

"I am very sure." She leaned forward and blew hard, so that her breath would penetrate the fabric.

"Then why . . . ?" His voice trailed off as she found an especially sensitive spot just below the joining of his thighs. He had to clamp his lips tight to keep from moaning.

She longed to hear that moan, to force sound from him— but knew too well the risk she took. Instead she let her fingers trail upward until they reached the buttons of his fall.

His hand came down to cover hers as she undid the first one. "I am really not sure that you should do this. You can still sneak back and reenter the box properly. No one will ever know."

"Is that really what you want?" She leaned forward and blew again, but this time she arched her back, pressing her breasts against the low neckline of her gown. "It's not what I want and I don't see why anybody will know anyway—unless you intend to be noisy."

"I am not sure I'll be able to contain myself."

"Oh, I think I can contain you." She grinned up at him and licked her lips in an exaggerated manner.

One of his hands released her and slid forward to caress the upper curves of her bosom. As always, his touch sent little sparks running through her and she had to bite her own lip not to moan. She raised her face and stared into his eyes as his fingers slipped under the lace edging of her dress, seeking ever more sensitive targets.

But it was his eyes that held her, that made the whole world disappear. His fingers were making her forget her own task, tempting her to give in to her own pleasure, but his eyes told her that her every pleasure was his, that all he wished was to make her happy—endlessly.

It was her turn to swallow and shiver.

She licked her lips not with exaggeration, but with pure emotion.

"I want to kiss you," he whispered, bending a little forward.

She pulled back, that much of her mind remaining. "No, that is impossible."

A breath ran through him like a shudder. "I know and it is the greatest torture that you could have thought of—to be stuck here, pretending to watch the singers—we are lucky they are loud—and all I want is to sink to the floor beside you, to push up your skirts and down your bodice, to bare you completely, to—."

Linnette shifted, uncomfortable as her body hummed to life. She pressed her thighs tight and ignored the dampness between them. His gaze might promise pleasure—but it was his turn.

She concentrated on his eyes again, watching as his pupils grew and darkened, feeling her power grow with his desire.

Picturing just what she wanted to do to him, letting that desire show clearly on her face, in her eyes, she arched her back further, settling her breasts firmly against him, pressing herself tight against his hardness. "If you use both your hands, you can push my bodice down, see my bare breasts, feel them against you."

He paused for a moment, and then freed her second hand, leaning forward just enough to follow her direction. "You planned this, wore this dress on purpose."

"I will confess that I had seduction in mind. After the way we left things this morning, I thought you might need some sweetening, but I was thinking of in my carriage later—and I wasn't even sure of that. I truly did not expect to find you at the opera. I was merely hoping that our paths might cross at some point later in the evening. I was even prepared to brave a few soirees and crushes looking for you."

"Such a courageous woman."

She laughed quietly, holding it deep in her throat, fully aware of his gaze being drawn back to her breasts as she knelt before him, her deep midnight dress the perfect background for her pale flesh. No, she had not planned this, but she would have, if she'd thought of it.

She let her fingers move toward each other, meeting at the center, surrounding him, caressing him through the fabric of his trousers.

He groaned—very softly.

She licked her lips, looking up at him from beneath lowered lashes. "Shh."

She pressed her fingers close, encircling him as best she could through the fabric, running her fingers back and forth, up and down.

And then her fingers were back on his buttons, pulling them loose, pushing down the fall, slipping inside his small clothes, baring him to her eager gaze.

Velvet and steel—she'd heard it a whispered description on several occasions, but never had it seemed as true as it did now. She licked her lips, again—this time without thought. He truly was everything she'd ever wanted.

"You are my every fantasy," he murmured, "and this, this is beyond even my most vivid dreams—pink-tipped breasts bare against my flesh, surrounding me, the fall of your curls, the silk of your dress. I wish you would see yourself through my eyes, see just how desirable you are, how unbelievable."

Sitting back slightly, settling herself more comfortably, she glanced at his face one more time, at the clenched jaw and rigid tendons in his neck, saw his fight for control. That would not last for long, not if she had any say in the matter.

She dropped her glance away from his face and settled it once again on his lower regions, on his full erection. God, he was beautiful. She'd never thought of the penis as beautiful— actually had always considered them rather funny—but there was nothing funny about his, about this moment.

She swallowed and ran her fingers up the tender flesh, and down—and up, stretching the soft skin over the steel interior.

A drop of moisture formed at the tip and she leaned forward, flicking it off with her tongue.

His whole body shuddered. She could feel the effort it took him not to cry out.

She flicked again, and again, before settling her lips firmly about the tip and sucking him in just a little.

His hands moved across her breasts, squeezing, tugging at the nipples. She bit back her own sigh. He knew her body too well. He caught her nipples between thumb and forefinger, pressing and releasing, moving in the small circles that could cause her to climax with no further contact.

Her belly tightened and clenched, flames of desire and pleasure rushing through her, tempting her to throw her head back and do nothing but enjoy.

The opera was rising to crescendo, the soprano reaching unheard-of notes.

She bent forward further, and licked, hard, firm, unrelenting. This was her moment, her power.

She felt the throb of the vein that ran along the underside, pulled back, ran her tongue up the vein and down again, running her fingers about the shaft, her tongue playing eagerly at the head.

She slipped one hand lower, reaching between his legs to fondle his balls. He might know her, but she knew him too, knew just what motion it took to drive him over the edge, to drive him to—.

He had died and gone to heaven—although he'd never imagined heaven to be a place of such torment. If Linnette kept moving at the pace she was, he'd be screaming before the aria was finished and wouldn't that be a fine thing.

Her lips closed about him again and he bit down on the inside of his cheek to hold in all sounds. She sucked steadily as her tongue danced about the lower side of his cock. He could feel the pressure building, the end coming—but she eased back again, looking up at him with that mischievous glint in her emerald eyes.

Her fingers were working magic on his balls, caressing and pulling, stroking, pressing.

God, it truly was heaven.

His head fell back. He hoped that the crowd would merely assume he was bored with the performance.

Her breasts were still beneath his hands and he played with the peaks, wishing he could grant her the pleasure she was giving him. She wiggled beneath his touch and he felt his own devilish desire to turn the table grow.

Once they were done, then he would have Linnette sneak out and then return. She could pretend she'd merely been refreshing herself. Then, when she was seated beside him, he could let his own hands do a little exploring. He wouldn't be able to taste her, but . . . Closing his eyes, he let his imagination run free as he thought of all the things he would love doing to her delectable body.

Her mouth was back on him and it drove most, but not all, thoughts from his mind. His fantasies of all the ways he would make her come, make her feel desire, the endless hours of pleasure—

—and then even that thought was gone. There was only sensation. Tightness. The endless drive to pleasure. He felt it start—knew release was near—knew there was no reason to hold back—his waiting would only increase her effort, increase the risk.

Forcing his hands from her breasts, he gripped the rails of the chair, pulled his head up to stare down at her—this miraculous woman, all cream skin, flashing hair, and blue silk, more than any man could ever want.

And then he was lost in her eyes, in her passion. He'd worried about not pleasing her, but her expression told a different story. Lips wrapped about his cock, eyes shining up at him—she was exactly where she wanted to be, where she needed to be.

She was his.

His forever.

God, it was too much.

She pulled deep, her tongue working its magic—and he was lost.

The orgasm grabbed him and held him, like none he could ever remember. He pumped into her, filling her, and she swallowed and licked, swallowed and sucked, driving him on even further.

He was surprised the roar did not rip from his chest, drawing all attention to him.

And still he came.

He watched her eyes growing larger, her body shook and strained along with his.

Her eyes filled him.

Then blackness.

Then a million flashes of light, the heavens colliding.

It was over.

He felt the collapse, felt his body sag upon the chair.

His eyes weighed heavy, but still he could not tear them from her. He felt more as if they were one person than two. He watched as she blew a long slow breath out, her cheeks shiny and pink from exertion. Her chest was rising and falling rapidly, and he could tell her heart raced.

And she looked happy. Damned happy.

He continued to hold her gaze and waited for her to speak.

Chapter Nine

She was happy. It was not a thought she'd ever had at such a moment—not that she'd ever had such a moment. She still couldn't believe that she'd done it.

And she couldn't believe that James was looking at her the way he was, as if she was the most perfect thing in the entire world, something he would give up everything for.

He'd had that look eight years ago on the night she'd first given herself to him and she'd never thought to see it again. Certainly never thought to believe it again.

But, she did believe it, believe him.

She let her mind mull over this fact as she continued to stare up at him, to stare into him. There was no deception in his gaze, only—only she did not dare to believe what it was she saw there, afraid that to even acknowledge the thought would make it fade, make it less real.

Her hands trembled slightly as she lifted them back to his lap and gave him a final caress before beginning to refasten his trousers. He lifted a lazy hand and tried to take the task from her, but she held strong, wanting to do this, to complete her role.

He allowed his hand to drop back and she finished, brushing all wrinkles from him, and pulling the edges of his coat forward, smoothing the fabric of his waistcoat. He looked like he'd been sitting, doing nothing more than enjoying the opera.

She was another matter, she was sure. Her hair must be a mess, her face flushed—and her gown, she leaned back and tried to arrange herself back into her bodice. It was not an easy task. Her corset had been pushed down and now held her breasts out in a ridiculous manner, rather like the prow of a ship. The lace edging of her gown lay flat and scrunched, and she didn't know what had happened to her pearls. She was sure she'd been wearing them at the beginning of the evening, hadn't she?

James watched her struggles with a most satisfied grin.

She stuck out the tip of her tongue at him and watched his eyes darken. She could read his mind, see him remember exactly what that tongue had been doing.

She blushed. She could feel the heat rise up her chest and knew her cheeks must be redder than ever. The realization only made her blush harder. She could perform fellatio at the opera with little embarrassment, but let James give her that look and she turned redder than a beet.

"Here, let me help you." His large hands reached into her dress and gave her corset a good pull, almost lifting her off the ground. Then he started to tuck—well, tuck and stroke—her breasts as he resettled them into her gown, his thumbs giving her nipples a last fondle.

When her cheeks heated this time, it was not from embarrassment. She looked down at herself as his long fingers finally pulled away from her heated flesh. "That is better, but I fear the lace will never be quite the same. My modiste would be mortified if she saw what I've done to her wonderful creation."

"I am afraid your hair is a little lopsided also. I'd try to fix it but I fear I'd only make it worse."

"Well, I suppose it can't be helped. I'll try to make it to the retiring room without being seen and then perhaps I can find a maid to help right it. I can make up some story for what happened to it."

She sat back on her knees and wondered what her skirts would be like when she stood. The floors were well swept, but the silk had definitely not been made for kneeling.

At least that was what she tried to think about. In truth, her whole mind was filled with the James and the conversation she knew they must have. Things had changed and there was no way to pretend they had not.

She didn't quite know what that meant, but talking with him was the only way to find out. There could be only honesty between them.

"I'd best be going. I know this aria and there is not much left." She kissed his kneecap, wishing she could reach his mouth, and he reached out one finger and stroked her lips. She kissed it, too.

She eased back slowly until she was once again against the wall and then slowly rose, keeping herself well hidden by the curtain. It was time to make her escape. Should she return or wait for him in her carriage? It was hard to decide which was more intriguing, sitting beside him, knowing what had just happened or the fast thrill of being alone in the carriage.

Before she could decide, before she could even move, there

was a sudden swish, and the curtains thrust open. "Well, my dear cousin, I am glad to have caught you before you left. I do hope I am not interrupting your enjoyment."

Linnette wanted to sink through the floor as Mr. Swatts strode into the box. How had he known? She settled for stepping back into the curtain, drawing it about her, not caring what the rest of the audience might think of the sudden billow of the fabric.

"No, not at all I was getting ready to leave myself." James stood as if to draw attention from her—and it seemed remarkably effective. Mr. Swatts did not even glance in her direction, his gaze only for James.

"I shall only delay you for a moment. I had planned to call on you at the hotel this afternoon, but I was informed that you had left."

"Yes, I am moving into my house in Mayfair."

He was? James had failed to mention that little tidbit to her, although admittedly she had not given him much time for discussion.

Mr. Swatts stepped further into the box, his attention still fully on James. "I should perhaps call on you there tomorrow, but I find the matter rather urgent. I am in need of twenty thousand pounds."

"And?" James's tone was remarkably even.

"And I think you should give it to me." Mr. Swatts took another step, swinging his walking stick.

James took a step forward, ascending the single step leading to the back of the box, bringing his height well over that of his cousin. "And why should I do that?"

"It would just be easier for all of us. I would hate to raise any challenge for the title. It would take years and might benefit neither of us."

Jaime stopped. "On what basis would you do that? I believe a thorough search was made before I was granted the title, before the trustees approved me. There is no question that it would go to you."

"That is only if you are who you claim."

"What?" James looked completely baffled and Linnette could only mirror the feeling.

"I've come across some men who were with you—or should I say with James Sharpeton—in Canada. They claim Mr. Sharpeton died of a bayonet thrust to his thigh in a battle near Niagara Falls. It seems unlikely, therefore, that you are Mr. Sharpeton."

Linnette thought of the long scar that marked James's upper thigh and hip. He'd never talked about it. Had it truly almost killed him? It was true there had been rumors of his death. She shuddered at the thought.

"I can assure you I am not dead," was James's only answer.

"And therefore, you cannot be Mr. Sharpeton. Do you think I have not noted that nobody in Town remembers you?"

"And why should they? I was so far removed from all this that I'd hardly been to London. I was a vicar's stepson, not some lordling. There is no reason that anybody would have noticed me before I inherited the title."

"My point exactly. It makes it very easy for you to pretend."

"And the duchess? She knew me in the past."

"And has every reason to pretend to know you now. In fact, I believe she was behind the scheme. The whole world knows that she has enjoyed handling the estate. Why should she not pretend her lover was the lost duke? And after that recent cartoon, the whole of society will believe you are lovers—everyone knows that she is not picky about who she takes to her bed."

What nerve! She'd been very picky, indeed. Swatts was just upset that she had refused him—and the rest of it was nonsense. She almost stepped forward to tell him so herself, when she saw James's hand form into a hard fist, every muscle of his arm tensed.

She waited.

And watched as he slowly relaxed the hand. When he spoke, it was with slow precision. "And she just happened to send me to Canada to be found?"

"I believe you were found in Boston. And perhaps you were there for your own reasons."

"And my stepfather and sister? Do you think they do not remember me?" James stayed in place, but Linnette could see his thighs tense with anger.

"And why have you not visited them? It does seem strange that you return after eight years abroad and there is no contact."

"I intend to visit as soon as matters of the estate are cleared up. And my stepfather is old and does not like to travel and so he has not come to London—but I assure you he will, if needed."

"And what will that prove? Doveshire holds the living at the vicarage and I believe it has just been granted to your sister's husband. I think they have plenty of reason not to want things changed. And I can assure you I would change things if I were granted the title—for both them and the dear dowager duchess. I think it really is best for us all if you just give me the money."

Linnette waited for James to say something, to threaten Mr. Swatts, to punch him, to scream—she didn't know what she expected, but something. Instead he stood as if frozen, holding himself back, only the clenching and unclenching of his fist betraying emotion.

Mr. Swatts seemed equally confused by the lack of reply. "So will you give me the money?"

James's chest swelled as he pulled in a deep breath. "Why do you need it?"

"What does that matter? Either you pay or I'll ruin both you and that tramp who thinks she is better than us all. I'll put her and then you in your places."

That was too much. She watched James coil like a spring, violence ready to be unleashed. He started to step forward, both hands now ready at his sides, but before he could reply another voice, a very feminine voice, burst into the discussion.

"This is all balderdash." Annabelle stepped forward. "Of course, he is who he says he is. Half his regiment was there to see him off. And they were distinctly calling him by name. My husband, the Marquess of Tattingstong, was there as well and can swear to it. Do you really think he thought to bribe a full company in Boston as part of his disguise? And as for the dowager duchess, if you ever speak ill of my friend again I'll see you driven from Town. You, sir," Annabelle turned to Mr. Swatts, "are a fool. And, I believe, a cheat."

Mr. Swatts turned as red as Linnette's dress. He thumped his stick up and down twice, his face flushed. A few words that no lady should know spewed from his lips. He stepped toward

Annabelle, stick raised—and then he took another look at James, saw the gleam in his eyes, saw James begin to raise a fist, and stepped back, hurriedly. "I'll speak to you later. This is not over," he said to James, then turned and strode from the box.

"Well, that was easier than I expected," James said as he leaned against the wall, his body relaxing, but a vein in his neck still pulsing. "Although somehow I doubt we have seen the last of him—and I actually hope that there is another encounter, one not at the opera. Perhaps a dark alley."

Annabelle ignored his final comment. "It is all rather silly. Of course, you are the duke. I don't know why people are always looking for elaborate plots. I always find life rather straightforward." Annabelle smiled slightly and turned to stare over at Linnette, still hiding in the curtains. "And I believe your pearls are under that seat—not lost in the drapery." She pointed to the chair that James had been sitting in. "They are what you are looking for, are they not?"

Linnette could only blush—again. She'd turned more shades of red this night than in all of her twenty-six years. She stepped forward, hoping not too many saw her magical appearance, and then walked back toward the pearls, which truly were lying beneath the chair. "Yes, of course, that's what I was looking for—what I came back for."

"I thought it must be." Annabelle's smile told a very different story than her words. "I thought I'd seen you leave, but your coach is still waiting—and I could not find you in the retiring room. I was going to talk to you about our discussion yesterday, and your earlier adventures at the park, but this does not seem like the time. Perhaps you can call on me tomorrow." She nodded to James and swept from the box.

"Well, my head is in a muddle. I am not sure whether I am coming or going. How can so much happen in so few hours?" Linnette asked as she checked the fastener on her pearls and then slipped them into her reticule. Her skirts really were hopeless, a complete wrinkled mess—and she was not even going to think about her hair.

James reached out to take her arm. "And what did happen in the park today? Somehow that bit of news became lost in everything else."

"That is what you want to talk about? All this happens and you want to talk about the park?"

No, he didn't want to talk about the park, but in truth, his mind was also a muddle and he didn't know what he was thinking beyond that he wanted to grab Linnette, get her alone in a carriage, and then figure it all out.

"You have ignited my curiosity. So, yes, tell me about the park."

She was still for a moment and then smiled that mischievous smile that drew him in every time. "I jumped in the lake— but that's not the story you'll hear from anybody else. And that's all I am saying here. I think we'd best escape or we'll be caught in the crowd at the end. If Annabelle saw my carriage, then it must be near the front."

"You what? The lake?"

"You heard me. Now come." She spun, her skirts flaring, and strode through the curtain. This time she did not return.

He followed, resisting the urge to whistle. It was an evening of highs and lows, but he had every expectation that it was going to end on a high—and the highs had been extremely high. He was still in awe at what Linnette had done—at the opera!

How did she move so fast? She was down the stairs and around the corner and he was still trailing in her wake. He had the sudden realization he'd be trailing in her wake for the rest of his days.

He hurried down the stairs after her. Rounding the corner he caught sight of her swaying hips and decided following her might not be so bad—the view was certainly fine.

Her carriage pulled up just as he exited the hall. How did she manage that? He'd taken a hack to avoid the tangle of coaches and everyone else seemed to wait for hours and she merely had to smile and her horses swept up. He would have asked her secret, but he had a feeling she'd just smile and shrug. She never had realized just how special she was.

Waving the groom away, he helped her into the carriage and followed after.

"We're alone." She said the words before the door was even closed.

"It's a sad state of affairs when the first thing that makes me think is that we can talk," he answered, his gaze dropping to her lips. They were red and slightly swollen, and despite his words he could not resist bending forward to lay the kiss he'd been longing for all evening upon them.

It was soft and sweet, connection rather than passion.

And then the flames flickered and grew, lips that had brushed now pressed, tongues began to taste and dance. He pushed Linnette back onto the bench seat, his hands circling her waist and holding her still. He plundered her mouth, his lips tight against her, his tongue circling her sweet, moist mouth.

For a moment it was perfect—and then her hands pressed hard against his chest. Her breath came in heavy pants, the heat prickling the hairs on his neck. "No, we really must talk first."

"Must we?"

She moved into a sitting position, slipping away from him. "Yes. You were right early this morning and I am right now. When we talk, it may bring anger, but afterwards—even if it takes hours to settle about me—I do feel closer to you."

"I am not feeling angry."

"No, I can tell." She let her eyes shift to his lap.

"Don't do that if you want to talk."

"Why didn't you pummel Mr. Swatts out of the box, if not off the balcony? I have never heard such nonsense."

James let out a long sigh. "It will sound silly—and in truth I did want to put the man's teeth down his throat. And when he spoke of you, I was ready to pummel him through the floor. I am not sure that he would still be living if Annabelle had not arrived." And he rather wished Annabelle had not arrived. His fists were still itching to make contact with Swatts's face.

"That I understand, but I am still not sure why you held back." She slid a little closer and laid a hand upon his shoulder. Passion flickered again, but he did his best to ignore it.

"I was hoping to slay a dragon."

"What?" She looked as if she had not the slightest idea of what he was talking about.

"When I asked how you could prove I was a man you could

trust, rely on, you told me to slay a dragon. I was hoping Mr. Swatts would be it."

"He's more of a snake than a dragon."

"And one without sharp fangs." James placed his hand over hers, engulfing it. "It sounds odd to say that I was hoping he really would present some threat. You had indicated that you feared I had returned for the title and not for you. I was seeking a way to prove that you were what I really wanted, that I would give up anything—even the title for you. I was hoping there would be a real battle. I was actually disappointed when Annabelle came in. It did ruin any potential for me to act a man. Although I fear Mr. Swatts could still create a stink if he wanted. People do like a good scandal. They don't always care about the truth of the matter. I would be tempted to pay the man simply to go away, but that would only make things look worse. And I have no faith he'd stay away. I'd hate to have him after me until the end of my days. Do you think a good thrashing would keep him quiet?" Did he sound too hopeful?

"We'll have to see about the thrashing. I am in general opposed to violence, but the man does ask for it. And you are right about the scandal. I think everybody will be watching us for months trying to decide the truth of the cartoon."

"I have a plan for that."

"You do?"

"Yes, but it will hold for a bit."

Linnette settled back in her seat but kept her hand on his shoulder, snug in his grasp. "Would you really have given up the title for me? Am I really more important?"

Chapter Ten

James's whole body went still beneath her touch. Linnette could see the deep thoughts swirling behind his eyes, but his words were simple. "I don't know," he said.

It was not the answer she wanted. She didn't pull her hand away, but it stopped its gentle stroke and caress.

And then he continued. "I am not sure that I prove I am a man to be relied on if I desert my responsibilities. If it were just the title, I would give it up—even to Swatts—in a moment. I don't think I will ever feel comfortable being a duke. I would even give the money away. I might not have had faith I could take care of you when I was twenty, but now I have every confidence in my own abilities. But, I do not know if I can let down all those who depend on me—and not just my father and sister. I cannot believe that Swatts would care for my tenants or for whether the fields were plowed or fallow."

It was her turn to sigh. "I must confess you are right about Swatts. Before you were found—when he still hoped to be the heir—he presented several ideas to me and they were all about turning a profit quickly. He had no care for the future."

"So the answer truly is that I don't know if I would give that

up, even for you. I fear I might if there were actually a choice."
He turned his whole body toward her. "I cannot live without
you Linnette. You are like opium in my blood, the slightest
taste gives me endless cravings. And not just for the sex, but
for you. I would wish to be with you even if all I could do was
breathe the same air."

"That does not sound healthy at all—but I do know the
feeling."

"Do you feel it too?"

His words forced her to answer, ready or not. "Yes, I feel it.
I am no longer sure that I can be without you. It seems strange
after two weeks that I should feel this way and I do worry that
it is just the passion. Can I really be in love again after eight
years?"

"I don't believe I ever stopped loving you, Linnette."

Now those were the words she wanted to hear. "I tried
to stop. I thought I had stopped. I would never have married
Charles if I had not thought I could stop, could forget you, but
now, now I wonder. I do fear you may be right."

"Is it really something to fear?" He bent over and slipped
his arms about her, lifting her onto his lap with ease.

She cuddled against his chest, feeling safe and oh so feminine. "I have been afraid of my feelings. As I said, I do not know
if I can trust you. I was so firm in that belief this morning and
I can only wonder in my change of opinion. I was so sure how
I felt, sure that I could never wed you. How can I be confident
in my feelings now?"

"And are you questioning? Do you trust me?"

She pulled back just enough that she could look into his
eyes again. "It is my turn to say 'I don't know.' I think I do

trust you. I want to trust. I want to have reason to trust. I, too, would have liked you to find that dragon to slay. And then when Swatts was speaking, I asked myself if that would really be trust, if I made you give it all up for me. Is it trust if something has been proved or is trust relying on someone when you do have doubts?"

His eyes crinkled. "I don't know."

"It is a dilemma. One I am hoping you will help me solve."

"Oh?" He snuggled her tighter, causing her to move across his lap, his increasingly interesting lap.

She wiggled a little to the side. That would come later. "Yes, I think I need to experiment, perhaps for a lifetime."

"And how would you do that?"

"I was thinking that if we lived together so I could see you every day, perhaps, god-willing, had a child or two, worked on managing Doveshire together, and kept talking, as well as kissing, that then in a decade or two I might know with more certainty if I could trust you." She dropped her gaze at the end, afraid of his answer, despite her own certainty.

"You are talking marriage?" His voice was gruff. "Do not play with me."

"I suppose I am. Although, I admit I seem to enjoy courting scandal these days. I believe that I would enjoy a long engagement—with us living in the same house. I'd like to hear the biddies talk about that one."

"Is that even possible?" He was stirring beneath her lap. He clearly liked the idea.

"I don't know." She smiled broadly as she said the words. "But I am certainly willing to find out. Mr. Swatts did mention you had left the hotel."

"Yes, I am not quite sure why I did it in such a hurry. But I felt a true need to be in the house."

"It might have forced me away."

"I've never seen you forced to do anything."

"You still haven't asked me—again."

"Asked you?"

"I may be forward and unforceable, but I do still believe it is your job to ask for my hand." She shifted her hips so his sex pressed firmly against hers. She knew just where this discussion should move—and fast.

But James evidently had other ideas. Before she could draw another breath, she found herself lifted and deposited on the seat while he slid to the narrow stretch of floor between the benches.

He took her hand in his and said the words—at least almost the words—she'd been hoping for. "Will you, Linnette Sharpeton, do me the honor becoming my wife? And don't think I didn't swear I was never going to ask again after this morning."

There was some temptation to roll her eyes. Would the man ever get over her laughter? "I would have been shocked if you hadn't sworn just as I swore I would never say yes."

"And is that a yes?" The man actually sounded unsure— and a little defensive.

"Yes. Yes. Yes." She bent down to give him a kiss and to draw him back up to her, but he continued to have ideas of his own.

He returned her kiss, but only lightly, before pulling back.

She was about to protest, but then his hands were under her skirts, rubbing her ankles, her calves, stopping for a lingering touch at the back of her knee—she loved that spot—then up her inner thighs. There was shiver of fresh air as he pushed her skirts up, baring her in the low light of the coach's lanterns.

"It's a good thing your skirts are already wrinkled," he said, bending his head to brush a kiss on each knee, and then letting his lips follow his hands as they worked their way up her thighs. "I was quite upset not to be able to taste you at the opera. It seemed most unfair. I intend to remedy that now."

"Oh—do—you?" Her voice squeaked at the end and he was only halfway up her thigh.

"Yes, I most definitely do, my dear wife-to-be." His tongue left slick lines across her inner thigh as it moved higher.

Speech became impossible. She swallowed, wanting to say more, but already lost in sensation. There would be more time for words later. And as his breath brushed her curls and his tongue targeted home, she didn't say a thing.

"So why did you jump in a lake?"

It was not a question he had ever imagined asking after sex, but as he lay back in Linnette's great bed, with a most satisfied woman in his arms, it occurred to him that it was the one question that had not been answered.

Linnette stiffened slightly, and then relaxed again, turning her face against his chest. "If you asked anyone, they would tell you that Elizabeth pushed me."

"That little—. I would have expected you to sound angry. It is unheard of to dump a lady in a lake." James shifted, trying to see her face.

In response to his movement, Linnette did turn her face up.

She smiled, but it did not quite reach her eyes. "That sounds almost Arthurian, but I am definitely no Lady of the Lake."

"Not swinging swords for vengeance?"

"As I said before, Elizabeth did not push me," she said the words very quietly, her breath warming his chest.

"But . . . ?"

"I truly did jump. She could not have stopped me if she had wanted to."

"Why?" He would never understand women, at least not this one.

"I just did. It seemed like a grand idea at the time, but now I fear I may regret it. It truly seemed more of a lark than anything—and a way to show that I was not hiding a belly under my skirts. Now I fear I should just have taken Annabelle's suggestion and thrown a masquerade and come dressed in drapery."

He said nothing as he considered her words. "Everyone thinks Elizabeth pushed you, but in truth you jumped. I am still not sure I understand why."

"I wanted to get back at her—perhaps I swung my sword of vengeance without thought. I certainly wanted sympathy for myself and for Elizabeth to face the consequences of what she's done with the cartoons, but now I am not so sure that I did anything but act like a spoiled child."

"I think I begin to understand." Although, in truth, he was not sure he did at all. He would have understood a punch or brawl, but to pretend to be pushed?

"No, you don't. But that is fine. I do not understand myself—although it did feel wonderful for a moment. And then I saw Kathryn and Annie and how they looked at Elizabeth. I did not want that. And then I ran into Annabelle and her sister as I left the park. They had seen the whole thing. Annabelle was full of sympathy for me, but something in her sister Lucille's gaze made me think that perhaps she saw me jump and knew I was a fraud. Lucille is quiet, but I have the feeling she sees everything."

"Will she say anything?"

"I do not know, and in some ways I hope that she does. I would deserve it—I warned you I was now courting scandal."

"That is nonsense—your deserving it, not the courting scandal. You are correct that I do not understand fully, but if Elizabeth is behind the cartoons, I cannot feel sympathy. She hurt you."

"I know—and yes, she did. But that is still no reason for me to act in such a fashion. We were good friends. It was never an easy friendship, true. But I think in many ways we are too much alike."

"I do not see that."

"We are both strong women whom the world has not always treated fairly, and yet we go on. I think perhaps that I have been luckier and she has resented me for that. I know I sometimes resent her ready tongue and wit—not that I am hurt by them, but that I am jealous of them. She always has the perfect reply and it seems that nothing upsets her, destroys her calm. At least not until today. She truly looked quite appalled as she stood there and I waded out, dripping."

"Was she angry?"

"Yes, but I saw respect also. It almost made me think she was not behind the cartoons, that it would have been beneath her. She has always been very straightforward in her actions. I think it is why I found this whole thing so surprising."

"Mmmm." It was not much of a reply, but his body was becoming very aware that Linnette was rolling her hips back and forth and it really didn't care about the cartoons any further. And his mind was beginning to think it just might agree.

Linnette began to plant lazy kisses along the underside of his chin, her tongue occasionally darting out to taste him. He pulled her higher, wanting to see into her eyes, wanting to know just how together they were in all of this.

She came along agreeably, more than agreeably, but then just before pressing her lips against his, she paused. "My only question is, if Elizabeth isn't behind the cartoons, then who is?"

THE MAIDS

"Oh, my God!!" Abby's voice echoed down the street.

Jane hurried up after her. Her friend had never taken the Lord's name in vain and it seemed most unlikely that it could mean anything but true disaster. "What is it? Is somebody hurt?"

"No, but look. I can't believe it. He would never do that to her. He's my favorite in the whole bloody bunch of them. Lady Tattingstong cannot deserve this. No, she cannot. Her husband is a true devil if this is true."

Jane found herself stopping beside her friend and staring at the chemist's window. Abby had sounded as if she were talking about a family member, not some lady they followed in cartoons and scandal sheets, but Jane did know the feeling. Following the lives of the duchesses had become a central part of her day.

And this cartoon truly was horrible. Lady Tattingstong stood in the front and slightly to the left. She was surrounded by bags of money, pound notes dripping out. That damned American flag stuck proudly out of her grand bosom. She smiled as if she controlled the whole world—and enjoyed it.

But behind her stood her husband, the marquess. Jane had come to know all of their faces well. He was looking at his wife, his expression one of distaste, even as he slipped his fingers forward and took several pound notes. That was not, however, the worst.

The worst was the pretty young woman held tightly in his other arm. The pretty young woman with a new baby in her arms. The pretty young woman whose bodice was stuffed full of Lady Tattingstong's pound notes. The pretty young woman who had another child beside her.

"My God," Abby repeated her earlier words. "The marquess has another family."

ABOUT THE AUTHOR

Most days Lavinia Kent loves her life and knows that she has found her own happily-ever-after with her husband and three children. But on those other days (you know which ones!), she is very glad for the wonderful romances, sensuous gowns, and tall, sexy men that fill her mind—and then her computer.

Lavinia lives in Washington, DC, with her family and an ever-changing menagerie of pets. She attended Wellesley College as an undergraduate and holds an MBA from Georgetown University.

What a Duke Wants is Lavinia's fourth book from Avon Romance. She also has a fun and, sexy serial of e-novellas, *The Real Duchesses of London*, available from Avon Impulse.

She can be contacted at her website www.LaviniaKent.com or through Facebook and Twitter.